Tighter . . . Tighter . . .

The snake wound itself even tighter around Michael's throat. *It's choking me!* he realized. Using both hands, he tried to pull it away, but the snake coiled itself tighter, tighter. Spots began to appear before Michael's eyes.

He tried to cry for help, but didn't have the breath. He felt himself growing weaker. *No*, he thought in horror. *No, no . . .*

Books by Lynn Beach

Available from MINSTREL Books

Phantom Valley™

Curse of the Claw

Lynn Beach

A MINSTREL® BOOK

PUBLISHED BY POCKET BOOKS

New York   London   Toronto   Sydney   Tokyo   Singapore

A MINSTREL PAPERBACK *ORIGINAL*

A Minstrel Book published by
POCKET BOOKS, a division of Simon & Schuster Inc.
1230 Avenue of the Americas, New York, NY 10020

Copyright © 1993 by Parachute Press, Inc.
Front cover illustration by Lisa Falkenstern

ISBN: 0-671-75927-2

First Minstrel Books printing February 1993

10 9 8 7 6 5 4 3 2 1

A MINSTREL BOOK and colophon are registered trademarks of Simon & Schuster Inc.

Phantom Valley is a trademark of Parachute Press, Inc.

Printed in the U.S.A.

Curse of the Claw

PROLOGUE

The cave appeared to be dark and empty to the man with the light at the entrance. The light was a burning torch. The man was dressed in animal skins, and around his neck was a long necklace made of bear claws. Bear claws were painted on his face and his arms.

Behind the man came more men dressed like him except that none of them wore a necklace. They all did have bear claws painted on their faces, though.

Two of these men carried between them a small statue of a bear carved out of black stone. On each of the bear's paws was one long, sharp claw. The expression on the statue's face was mean and dangerous.

The man with the necklace moved inside the cave and began to carve a hole in the back wall. While he worked, the other men chanted in their native language.

When the leader finished digging, he joined the other men in chanting.

Carefully then, they picked up the statue of the bear and put it in the nook.

As they set it down, there was a flash of red light, and the cave filled with a loud roaring. It sounded like the roaring of a bear, but this was even louder than thunder.

For a moment the statue glowed, and the long claws glittered in the red light. Now the man with the necklace began to talk to the other men. He talked to them in their ancient language. All the men shook in fear when they heard what their leader was saying.

When he finished speaking, there was another flash of light and roaring again filled the cave.

Frightened, the men all left.

Alone in the dark, the statue of the bear stood in its nook. It stood and waited through the seasons, through snow, through sunlight, through rain and wind. The climate began to change, and then the land did, too. Brave travelers came to the valley and settled there. Still the bear remained hidden in the cave. Hundreds of winters turned into hundreds of springs before anyone entered the cave again.

CHAPTER 1

"WHAT do you mean, you're leaving Chilleen?" Jennifer May reined her pony in and stared at her friend Michael Cullen.

"It's not definite," said Michael, trying to smile. He patted his pony, Duke, on the side of the neck. "It's just that my scholarship runs out at the end of this spring term."

It was a warm afternoon, and the friends were riding on a trail in the woods near Chilleen Academy, where they were both students. Jennifer had wanted to talk Michael into taking the same classes as she was in the fall.

Jennifer's thick sandy hair bounced under her helmet as she shook her head. "But you make good grades," she said. "Can't you get another scholarship?"

3

"I thought so," said Michael. "But it turns out all the scholarships for next year have been awarded. According to Mr. Elias there's no money for more scholarships. I was too late applying." Michael stared past Jennifer at the thick forest around them. He couldn't imagine giving up Chilleen and the Southwest to return to his old school in Indianapolis. He wanted to stay in Phantom Valley with his friends. Back through the trees, he could see the school's rustic main building.

"Bummer," said Jennifer. "Is that why you've been sort of weird and quiet lately?"

"I'm always weird," Michael joked. Removing his helmet, he ran his hands back through his short black hair and crossed his eyes to make Jennifer laugh. He felt funny talking about his money problems to her. He'd been worried for a few weeks. Somehow it hadn't seemed that serious, that real, till he mentioned it to her.

Jennifer was silent for a moment as if thinking about something. "What do your parents say? Can they help you any more?" she finally asked.

Michael didn't answer at first. His parents were happy he was at Chilleen, but private school was expensive, and he had three older brothers in college. He knew his family couldn't afford to help him more than they were already. "I don't think so," he said.

"Well, we'll have to think of something," said Jennifer. "I mean, I'm not going to let you go back to Indianapolis—now that I've trained you to race your horse."

Michael grinned at her. Jennifer always tried to see

the bright side of things. "Come on," he said. "Once we get out of the woods I'll race you back to the stables."

Remembering what Jennifer had taught him, Michael fastened his helmet, then leaned forward on Duke and dug his knees into the pony's flanks. Duke broke into a trot, then a canter, and finally a gallop. The two friends ended up back at the stables—at the exact same time.

"Today we're starting a unit on American writers," said Mr. Carver, Michael's English teacher. "We'll be using a different textbook. Maria and Diane, will you please pass them out? Remember to sign the checkout slip and put your name in the front of the book."

Michael took his copy of the heavy orange-covered book and opened it to the inside of the front cover. He saw that two students had had the book before him, a Billy Merina and a Linda Anne Rogers. He had never heard of either of them and decided they must have already graduated. He signed his name below theirs and flipped through the book.

As Mr. Carver talked, Michael continued to turn pages. About two-thirds of the way through the book, he was surprised to find a piece of paper.

That's funny, he thought to himself. The piece of paper was only slightly smaller than the textbook pages, but it was yellow and crinkled, as if it was very old. At first Michael thought someone had used the sheet as a bookmark. But when he tried to pull it out, he saw that it was sewn into the book, like the other pages.

How strange, he thought. *The bookbinder must have made a mistake when the book was printed.* Michael studied the yellowed page. The heading, in curly old-fashioned black letters, read: *Book of the Spirits.* The text started in the middle of a sentence. ". . . a curse that brings great danger," it said. There were several blank lines, and then in the middle of the page, in the same curly letters as in the heading, were the strange words: *"Teglet halaluk adiras nanidoglu mya teglet."*

Michael almost laughed. What in the world could that mean? he wondered. It wasn't any language he'd ever heard. He raised his eyes to the front of the room where Mr. Carver was busy writing on the blackboard.

Whispering, Michael repeated the strange words out loud. *"Teglet,"* he said. *"Halaluk. Adiras. Nanidoglu. Mya. Teglet."*

As soon as he finished saying the words, the room became darker, as if a cloud had passed over the sun. Michael blinked, and the darkness grew deeper. He felt something invisible push against him, like a wind. Then without warning he became dizzy. The room began spinning around with him in it. His heart started to pound heavily, and it became hard for him to breathe. The wind was taking his breath away. Just as the darkness seemed ready to become total, he heard a deep roaring, so loud that it made his ears ring. An instant later the wind, the darkness, and the roaring were gone—all at once.

Michael took a deep breath and glanced around the room. Everything seemed to be normal. Mr. Carver was writing a time line on the blackboard, and the other kids were taking notes. He turned to the window, expecting to see storm clouds. The sky was bright blue and cloudless. He turned his attention back to the classroom, puzzled. No one else seemed to have noticed what had just happened.

Michael started to ask Kim Harris, who was sitting in front of him, if she'd heard the roaring. Before he could say anything a sudden loud buzzing took his attention. A big black wasp was swooping down at him, dive-bombing his head.

"Eww!" Kim cried, turning around in her seat. She jumped up from her desk. "It's a wasp!"

"Swat it!" cried Randy Moser from the next row.

Michael picked up his notebook and swatted at the wasp, but it easily flew out of the way. He got out of his seat and moved around to the far side of the room. The wasp followed him.

"It's after Michael!" someone called out, laughing.

Michael swatted at the wasp again, but the insect dived straight at him. He felt a sudden sharp sting on the side of his neck. "Stop it!" he yelled, slapping at the insect.

"Mr. Cullen!" Mr. Carver cried, worried. "Are you all right?"

"I'm fine," said Michael. "Except that wasp just stung me."

Mr. Carver crossed to the back of the room and examined Michael's neck. "How very odd," he said. "You'd better go see the nurse."

"I'm okay," said Michael.

"You can't be sure," said Mr. Carver. "Many people have allergic reactions to insect stings. Run along, now. One of the other students will give you your assignment for tomorrow."

Embarrassed, Michael gathered up his books and left the classroom annex and headed across the lawn to the main building where the infirmary was. *Why do these things always happen to me?* he wondered. *Eighteen kids in the class, and the wasp picks* me *to sting.*

He had almost reached the main building when he was startled by a sudden rustling sound from one of the bushes in front of the porch. Michael turned to see what was making the sound. To his surprise something small and brown darted out of the bush and headed straight toward him.

"Hey!" he yelled. He dodged and fell onto the steps. His hand flew out to break his fall. At that very instant a small brown sparrow jabbed its beak into the fleshy part of his hand between the thumb and forefinger.

"Ow!" Michael cried. Angry and upset, he shook the bird off. The sparrow flew toward his head, chattering as if it were angry. Then abruptly it turned and headed back to the bush. Michael looked down at his hand. A drop of blood was beginning to ooze from the spot where the bird had pecked him.

CURSE OF THE CLAW

I don't believe this, he thought. *Two animals have attacked me in the last five minutes*. He made sure the sparrow was gone before he started up the steps. At least this would make a funny story to tell Jennifer, he told himself. His neck was stinging, and his hand had begun to throb. *Maybe*, he decided, *it's not so funny after all*.

CHAPTER 2

BY lunchtime Michael had almost forgotten about the wasp and the sparrow. Mrs. Albert, the nurse, had put a Band-Aid on the bird bite and some soothing salve on the wasp sting. "I don't know how this happened, Michael," she'd said. "But you should try to be more careful."

Michael protested that he *had* been careful, that the animals had attacked him for no reason at all.

Standing in the lunch line, he began to scratch his wasp bite before remembering that Mrs. Albert had said not to touch it. He ordered the day's special, macaroni and cheese, then carried his tray to a table and slid in beside his roommate, Luke Tremont. A moment later Jennifer brought her tray over. She sat down on the other side of the table, next to their friend Chubber Dunbar.

"I don't believe you guys," Chubber said, eyeing his three friends' loaded trays. "How can you can eat so much and stay so skinny?"

"We don't eat half as much as you do," said Luke. "You're the only person I ever saw eat a whole pizza."

"I couldn't help it," said Chubber. "It was pepperoni, my favorite."

"You don't seem to be eating much today, Chub," said Jennifer, pointing at the half-eaten portion on his plate. "On a diet?"

"Of course not," said Chubber. "I'm just not in the mood for this mystery meat and macaroni. It tastes horrible."

"Mystery meat is right," said Luke, pushing his food around his plate. "What is this stuff, anyway?"

Jennifer took a big bite of hers, then made a face. "According to the menu it's meat loaf," she said. "But it doesn't taste like any meat loaf I ever had."

"I read that in some countries in Asia they make meat loaf out of insects," said Luke.

"Gross!" said Jennifer, pushing her tray away.

"Aren't you going to eat your brownie?" asked Chubber, reaching toward her tray.

"Go ahead," said Jennifer. "I've lost my appetite!"

"Seriously," said Luke. "The food has been really bad lately. If Chubber won't eat it, you know it has to be *really* gross! Have you guys noticed?"

"Now that you mention it," said Jennifer.

"Didn't you hear?" said Chubber. "We've got a new cook."

"You're kidding," said Jennifer. "What happened to Mrs. White?"

"She had some kind of family problem," Chubber said. Michael looked at his friend and smiled. Chubber always managed to know the latest news about everyone on the Chilleen campus.

"So who's the new cook?" asked Luke.

"All I know is that his name is Mr. Grady," answered Chubber. "I don't know where he came from, but I can tell you he hasn't been a chef for very long. I saw him looking up in a cookbook how to make oatmeal the other morning."

"You mean you were spying on him?" asked Jennifer.

"Not exactly spying," said Chubber. "But I thought I ought to check him out. To me, the cook is the most important person at Chilleen."

Jennifer laughed. "He must be a really bad cook if he needs a recipe for oatmeal."

"I think he's just starting out," said Chubber. "He probably just got out of cooking school or something."

"I'll tell you something," said Luke. "I have a feeling the guy took the wrong job."

"What do you think, Michael?" Jennifer asked. "How's your macaroni?"

Michael looked down at his plate. He realized he'd been eating the macaroni without tasting it. "Okay," he said.

"Are you feeling all right?" Jennifer asked.

"Sure I am," said Michael. "Why?"

"You haven't said anything since we sat down," she said. "And, hey—what happened to your hand?"

Michael glanced down at the bandage. He thought about telling his friends what had happened with the sparrow and the wasp, but he realized how silly it would sound.

"Nothing," he said. "I just got a paper cut, that's all."

By the next morning, Saturday, the wasp sting had stopped itching, and the bird bite didn't hurt at all. Michael figured it had just been one of those strange things.

He was deciding which shirt to wear when Luke came into the room from the hall. His short red hair was still wet from his shower, but he was all dressed. "Hey, roomie," he said. "Ready for our movie in Silverbell?"

"Just about," said Michael. "I have to finish up my history homework first."

"Well, hurry up," said Luke. "I've already got our off-campus passes. I'll meet you back here around noon."

As always, Silverbell was lively on a Saturday afternoon, filled not only with townspeople but with families and workers from neighboring ranches and the Native American reservation. There was a fairly long line for the movie, but Michael didn't mind. He liked to watch all the people in the town square as they strolled around, buying things out of the booths lining the paths or watching artists at work.

The line moved slowly, but finally the boys reached the front. Michael gave Luke his money and stepped out of the line while his friend bought the tickets. While he was waiting, Michael heard a rustling behind him. Curious, he turned to see that he was standing beside a nearly full trash can. The rustling was coming from inside the can. *That's weird,* he thought. He raised his eyes to the trees. There was no wind. The sound inside the can became louder. It sounded almost frantic, as if something was inside trying to get out.

A little nervous, Michael stepped away from the can. The papers at the top of the can moved, and a small gray mouse appeared. It jumped out of the trash can, ran down the side, and, before Michael could move, started running up the leg of his jeans.

"Hey!" Michael shouted, startled. He reached down to brush the mouse off—and the mouse opened its little jaws and nipped at him. Michael shook his hand hard, and the mouse fell onto the sidewalk and scampered away.

His heart hammering heavily, Michael just stared at the small red spot where the mouse had nipped him. *It's just like the wasp and the sparrow,* he thought. *The mouse attacked me—for no reason at all.*

★　　★　　★

The mouse bite ached all day long, but by early Sunday morning the tiny spot was gone.

Chubber was standing impatiently in Michael's doorway. "Come on," he said. "Are you ready?"

Michael nodded sleepily. He and some of the other first-year kids were going on a nature hike with Mr. Rothrock, the biology teacher. It was early spring and hiking season was just starting.

"Will you hurry up?" said Chubber. "They're going to leave without us."

Michael glanced at his watch. Chubber was always worried about time. "Just one more thing," he said. He reached into a dresser drawer and removed a can of bug repellent. *This ought to protect me,* he thought. *From insects, anyway.*

The school van was standing in the circular driveway. The other students going on the hike were already there, dozing on the grass, enjoying the early-morning spring sun.

After a moment Mr. Rothrock came out of the main building with a tall, overweight gray-haired man. "This is Mr. Grady," he told the students. "Some of you already know he's the new cook. It's his day off, and he asked to come along to learn more about Phantom Valley."

Mr. Grady got into the front seat of the van with Mr. Rothrock, while the kids all piled into the rear seats. Michael and Chubber sat in the very last seat, which was turned to face out the back window.

"So that's Mr. Grady," said Michael once the van started up. "No wonder he's a cook. He obviously likes to eat."

Chubber laughed. "There's nothing wrong with eating," he said. "I was talking to him the other night," he went on. "He's a really nice guy. He said I can have snacks any time I want them."

"Are you sure you want them—the way he cooks?"

"He told me this was his first cooking job," said Chubber. "I'm sure he'll get better."

"Yeah, maybe," said Michael. "I just wish he'd done his learning before he came here."

Wild Horse Canyon was located between the academy and Silverbell. Although Michael had explored some areas around Chilleen Academy, he'd never been to Wild Horse Canyon before.

"This is great," said Chubber as they piled out of the van.

"I know," said Michael. "And it's a perfect day for climbing."

Michael moved away from the van and tilted his head way back to look up at the tops of the cliffs. The area was wild, with red rock cliffs and patches of dense bushes and pine trees.

"This is one of the less-explored areas in Phantom Valley," Mr. Rothrock explained as they started up an old steep trail. "No one has ever lived around here. It's said that even the ancient Native Americans avoided the area."

"Why's that?" asked Chubber.

"No one really knows," said Mr. Rothrock. "There's very little water most of the year. And the legends say the canyon is haunted."

At his words, Michael inspected the area more closely. It wasn't hard to believe there were legends about its being haunted. The cliffs were steep and craggy, and strange-shaped boulders were strewn everywhere. It had probably looked just this way when the ancient Native Americans first came here, he thought.

As they began to climb, Michael had the uncomfortable feeling that something was watching him. Once or twice he swung his head around, but he saw nothing out of the ordinary. He did notice a black hawk circling lazily in the bright sky. In fact, the large bird seemed to be flying directly over his head now, swooping lower and lower. Michael glanced around nervously, but the other kids didn't seem to notice the hawk. He decided not to say anything and kept climbing.

"Hey, look," said Chubber, suddenly pointing to the cliff face above them. "Is that a cave?"

Michael squinted against the bright light. On the side of the cliff they were climbing, thick brush was growing along a ledge. Hidden behind the brush was a dark indentation in the rocks. "I think you may be right," he said. "Let's go check it out."

"Are you kidding?" asked Chubber. "Only a fly could get over there."

"No," said Michael. "It won't be hard. Look at that ledge. I see handholds all the way across."

Chubber glanced up as the other students followed Mr. Rothrock and Mr. Grady around a bend in the path. The teacher couldn't even see that Michael and Chubber had stopped climbing.

"Don't worry," said Michael. "We can catch up before anyone even knows we're missing. Mr. Rothrock said they'd rest at the top. We'll catch them there."

"I don't want to miss out on any snacks," said Chubber.

"Chill out, will you?" Michael said. "It'll just take a few minutes."

"I don't know why I let you talk me into these things," said Chubber with a sigh. He began to follow Michael across the ledge toward the opening.

Michael was in the rock-climbing club at school, and the climb to the cave was even easier than it had first appeared. The ledge was wide and solid, with several pieces of rock jutting out as handholds. Five minutes later he'd reached the opening.

"You were right," he told Chubber. "It *is* a cave. It looks pretty big, too."

Cautiously he stepped inside. The cool air felt almost as if the cave were air-conditioned.

"This is great," said Chubber, once they were inside. "I thought it would be all dark and spooky."

"I think it's bright because the sun's shining right on

the mouth of the cave," Michael said. "It's got to be a lot darker at other times of the day. Come on, let's explore the place."

He began to circle the cave, keeping an eye out for any sign that anyone had been there. Except for some bat droppings, the cave seemed as if it had been empty since the beginning of time.

"This is neat," Chubber said. "But we'd better get back on the trail. Mr. Rothrock will notice we're gone."

"Just a minute," Michael said. "I want to see what's in the back." He inched his way to the very back of the cave, where it was much darker. There was something strange about the back wall. It wasn't completely smooth like the other surfaces. Curious, he stepped even closer. Laying his hand on the rock, he found a hollowed-out niche. It was about the size and shape of a shoe box and seemed to be man-made rather than natural. Michael frowned, puzzled, before reaching out and running his hands around the inside of the niche. When he touched it, it seemed to glow, as if someone were shining a light on it.

"Hey, Chubber," he called. "I think I found—"

His words were cut off by a sudden deep, hollow roar. It was as loud as thunder overhead. Michael felt the hair on the back of his neck stand up as he realized he'd heard the noise before.

It had been in the classroom the other day just before the wasp attacked him.

"Chubber!" he cried. "Chubber, do you hear—"

"I don't hear anything," said his friend, slightly annoyed. "Now come on. Let's get back."

Michael was still hearing the hollow echo of the terrifying roar. A moment later the entire cave went black.

CHAPTER 3

"**C**HUBBER!" Michael couldn't keep the panic out of his voice. "Are you all right?"

"What happened?" Chubber cried at the same moment. "The light's gone—"

"Excuse me!" interrupted a deep voice. As Michael watched, light reappeared at the front of the cave. Now he saw, standing beside the entrance, the large form of Mr. Grady.

"Mr. Grady!" Chubber said. "Your body cut off all the light for a minute! You scared us."

"What are you doing here?" Michael blurted out.

"I could ask you the same question," said Mr. Grady. "Aren't you supposed to be with the others?"

"We just wanted to explore a bit," said Michael.

"Well, I'm sorry if I startled you," the heavy man said. "But I think you'd better get back to the others."

"All right," said Chubber, turning to leave the cave.

Michael followed his friend, then noticed that Mr. Grady was staying behind. "Mr. Grady?" he called. "Aren't you coming?"

"You boys go on," said the cook. "I have some things I want to look at in here."

"That's funny," said Michael when he and Chubber had gotten back on the trail again.

"What is?"

"What Mr. Grady said," Michael answered. "What could he want to look at in that cave?"

"See you at dinner," Chubber said when the boys got out of the van back at the academy. "I've got to work on my math."

Michael knew he should do his homework, too, but he wasn't in the mood. It was still early, so he decided to bike over to see Jennifer. Her family lived near the school, so she was a day student and went home every night. He signed out, unlocked his bike, and started pedaling north.

The sky was sparkling blue as Michael sped along the side of Silverbell Road. A quarter mile from the school he came to a narrow road and turned his bicycle east toward Jennifer's father's ranch.

The road was dusty but smooth. It was slightly downhill to Jennifer's house, so Michael began to pedal as hard as he could, to see how fast he could go.

By the time Michael could make out Jennifer's house

as a speck in the distance, he was going so fast he felt as if he were flying.

Suddenly a blur appeared beside his bike, at the side of the road. One quick glance showed him it was a large jackrabbit with giant ears.

Weird, he thought.

The jackrabbit kept pace with him, and now it was moving closer toward him. Michael got a sudden feeling of dread in the pit of his stomach. *No*, he thought. *Not the rabbit, too.*

He began to pedal harder. The rabbit continued after him, moving closer and closer to the back wheel. It was only a couple of inches from the wheel now.

Michael started to swerve to pull away, but at that moment another jackrabbit, even larger than the first, suddenly ran across the road in front of his bike.

"No!" he screamed. He turned the wheel to miss the rabbit, but he was going too fast. The bike spun out of control on the soft dirt, and he flew over the handlebars and through the air.

He put his arms out and landed hard on his hands and knees, then rolled over onto his side. Michael lay there trying to catch his breath for a moment before he saw the two rabbits coming toward him.

"No!" he cried. "Go away! Get away!" He picked up a rock and threw it. One of the rabbits bounded off, but the other kept coming, its teeth bared like those of a dog.

"Get away!" Michael screamed again. He picked up

another rock and threw it, then grabbed his bike and climbed on. He pedaled as fast as he could, and when he finally looked back, both rabbits were gone. He kept riding as fast as he could until he was in Jennifer's front yard.

"Hi, Michael!" she cried, running out of the house. "I saw you riding. I never knew you could ride so fast."

"Neither did I," Michael gasped. His heart was pounding hard. "Can I have a glass of water?" he asked when he had his breath back.

"Sure," she said. "Come on in."

Michael followed her into the kitchen and drank two glasses of cool water.

"What's going on?" she said. "Why were you riding so fast? Is something wrong?"

"I don't know," Michael said. "I mean—yes, there's something wrong. But I don't know what."

Jennifer just looked at him.

"It all started on Friday," he said. And then he told her everything that had happened, from the time the wasp stung him in English class. "They all attacked me," he finished. "The wasp and the bird on Friday, the mouse on Saturday, and now a rabbit."

Jennifer continued to stare at him, and then her face broke out in a smile. "Great story," she said, laughing. "For a moment I almost believed you."

"It's not a joke!" Michael exclaimed. "It's all true! Everything that happened is true!"

"Right," she said. "Sparrows and rabbits are totally harmless."

"But—" Michael stopped. "Oh, what's the use?" he said.

"Come on," said Jennifer. "I've got a new Nintendo game. That'll take your mind off—off whatever's bothering you." She led Michael into the den, which was downstairs.

She opened the door, and Michael began to relax when he saw the familiar wood-paneled room with its black leather furniture.

"It's a neat game," Jennifer said. "I've only gotten up to level—" Her words were cut off by a terrified-sounding screech. Both friends turned toward the sound.

Horrified, Michael watched Jennifer's old tabby cat, Pumpkin, suddenly uncoil from the couch. Hissing and yowling, the cat launched itself into the air, its claws aimed directly at Michael's face.

CHAPTER 4

"**Y**OWWR!" screamed the cat.

Michael ducked just in time to escape the sharp, deadly claws.

"Roawrrr!" the cat yowled. Its back was arched and it was staring at Michael as if he were a dog or some other enemy.

"Pumpkin!" Jennifer cried. "Stop it! What's gotten into you?"

The cat crouched, ready to attack again.

"Get her out of here!" Michael cried.

It was too late. The cat sprang again, sinking its claws into Michael's jacket.

"Hey!" he yelled. "Cut that out! It's me, Pumpkin! Michael! I'm your friend!"

The cat continued to dig her claws into him, spitting and hissing.

Horrified, Jennifer pulled the cat off her friend. The cat struggled and jumped out of Jennifer's arms to dart under a table.

"Come on, Pumpkin!" cried Jennifer. She got down on her hands and knees. "Come on, puss!" She was beginning to sound angry. Quickly she reached under the table and scooped up the little animal. Then she carried her, howling and hissing, out of the den.

"I don't believe this!" Jennifer said, slamming the door on the cat.

"It's just what I told you," said Michael. "For some reason, all the animals in Phantom Valley have turned against me."

"But why?" said Jennifer. "I mean, it doesn't make any sense. Are you using some kind of weird new soap or something?"

"No," said Michael. "I'm using all the same things. Nothing is different. I can't figure out what's going on."

"Well, something must have changed," said Jennifer. "Animals can sense things we can't. There's got to be something about you, or something you've done, that's spooking them."

"I haven't done anything." Michael sank down onto the sofa, discouraged and frightened.

"Think," said Jennifer, sitting beside him. "There

must be something. Something strange, or something different that's happened."

"Nothing, really," said Michael. Then he remembered—it seemed like such a little thing, but— "The other day in English class," he said, "we got new books. Mine had a page from another book bound in it by mistake. On the paper were all these strange words. When I read them out loud the room got dark, and I heard this weird roaring noise."

"You what?"

"I know it sounds crazy," said Michael, "but that's what happened. And right after that, the wasp stung me."

For a moment Jennifer didn't answer. She looked as if she was thinking hard about something. "Are you sure the wasp got you *after* you said the words?"

"Of course I'm sure."

"And you didn't do anything else? Nothing strange?"

"No," said Michael. "I told you."

"Well," said Jennifer after a moment. "That must be it."

"What must be it?"

"The words," Jennifer went on. "Somehow the words made it happen."

"Wow," said Michael, sitting and taking in what Jennifer had said. "What if it is true? If the words somehow did cause the attacks, what can I do about it now?"

"I don't know," said Jennifer. "The first step is to find out more about those words. Come on, let's go back to school and check out your book again."

Michael waited on the front porch while Jennifer asked her father to give them a ride to school. Jennifer's family had an old-fashioned porch swing, and he was going to sit in it to wait. From the corner of his eye, he noticed something on the swing move just before he sat.

He looked closer and gasped as he recognized a small straw-colored scorpion. He knew that small scorpions were the most dangerous. He crossed to the far side of the porch to find something he could use to deal with the scorpion.

The scorpion had jumped off the swing and was moving across the porch toward him.

Quickly Michael stepped off the porch into the front yard. Moving so fast it was a blur, the scorpion ran off the porch and into the grass, heading straight for Michael.

It's chasing me! he thought in panic. The scorpion was so small he could barely see it. It was just a movement in the grass. He ran to the back of the house and stopped, panting. He looked around, but there was no sign of the scorpion.

When he got back to the front of the house he was relieved to see Mr. May and Jennifer loading his bike into the back of their pickup truck.

"Hi there, Michael," said Mr. May.

"Hello, Mr. May," said Michael.

"Where've you been?" asked Jennifer. "I thought you were going to wait for me on the porch."

"I'll tell you later," said Michael. Keeping a careful eye on the ground, he stepped into the cab of the pickup. Only when the truck had turned onto the road did he feel safe.

While he drove, Mr. May talked about some cattle he'd been trying to find, but Michael scarcely listened. All he could think about was what had happened with the animals. Till then it had seemed almost funny, even the attack by Jennifer's cat. Scorpions were a different matter. They were dangerous—their sting could kill. Whatever was happening, Michael realized, was no joke—it was serious. Deadly serious.

Michael was glad that Luke wasn't in their room. He didn't feel like explaining the whole thing to another person. He pulled his English book from the shelf above his desk. "This is it," he said, showing the book to Jennifer.

"It looks like a completely ordinary book," she said.

"It is," Michael agreed. "Except for the page that doesn't belong." He opened the book to that page and showed it to her.

"*Book of the Spirits*," she said, reading the title on the page. "Strange name." She ran her hands over the page. "This paper feels really weird," she said. "Not like ordinary paper at all."

Michael touched the paper too. It felt old and crinkly, not like any paper he'd ever handled.

Jennifer quickly read the page. " 'A curse that brings great danger,' " she read aloud. "Are these the words you said?" she pointed to the strange words in the middle of the page.

"Don't say them!" Michael cried, snatching the book out of her hands. "The same thing could happen to you!"

"Don't worry," said Jennifer. "What's on the other side of the page?"

"I don't know," said Michael, realizing he'd never bothered to turn the page. He turned it now. On the other side was a picture of a bear's paw with a single long, curved claw. Beneath the picture was writing.

" 'The only way to stop the curse,' " Jennifer read aloud, " 'is to recite this ancient chant. The following words must be proclaimed in a loud voice.' " After the words there was an arrow pointing to the next page.

"Where's the rest of it?" Michael asked.

"There is no next page," said Jennifer. "Do you think it could be somewhere else in the book?" She began to flip through the pages, checking for another page that didn't fit. There was nothing that didn't belong, nothing that didn't have to do with American authors. Disappointed, she turned back to the original page.

"I've got to find it!" Michael cried. "I've got to find the next page so I can stop the curse."

"But how? It could have been bound in some other book."

"I don't think so," said Michael. He pointed to a ragged triangle of yellow paper right behind the first full page. "This jagged piece is the same kind of weird paper. The page was here all right," he told Jennifer. "But it's been ripped out!"

CHAPTER 5

"YOU'RE right," said Jennifer. "So the next page must have been in this book originally. But how will we find it?"

"I don't know," answered Michael. Could these weird things really be happening to him because of a curse? And if they were, how would he ever find the words to stop the curse? He looked again at the pictures, first the one of the bear, then the close-up of the claw. "What do you suppose this means?" he asked, pointing at the claw.

"I don't know," admitted Jennifer. "It looks like the claw of some animal. Maybe of the bear on the other side of the page." She flipped the page back, and they looked at the bear on the other side.

"What could the bear have to do with the curse?"

Michael wondered out loud. "The only things that have attacked me have been insects or small animals."

"There's only one way to find out," said Jennifer. "We've got to find that missing page."

"But how?" said Michael. "The pages weren't supposed to be in the book in the first place. The other page could be anywhere—anywhere in the world!"

"Maybe whoever had the book before you tore the page out and kept it," Jennifer said.

"Maybe," Michael agreed. "But how could I find—" Then he remembered that two people had had the book before him. They'd signed their names inside the front cover. Excited, he flipped to the inside of the front cover. "Here are the names of the kids who had the book before me," he told Jennifer. "Maybe one of them knows what happened to the page."

"Let's see," said Jennifer. "Linda Anne Rogers and Billy Merina," she read. "I've never heard of Billy, but Linda Anne's family lives in Silverbell. My cousin used to take riding lessons with her."

"Great," said Michael. "Let's give her a call."

They looked up Linda Anne in the Silverbell directory, then went to the pay phone at the end of the hall.

"Hello?" said a gruff man's voice.

"Hello," said Michael. "Is this the Rogers residence?"

"Who?" said the man.

"Is this 555-1612?" said Michael.

"That's right," said the man. "The Rogers family doesn't live here anymore. They moved away over a year ago."

"Oh, no," said Michael. "Do you know where they went?"

"No," said the man. "They didn't leave a forwarding address."

For a moment Michael couldn't think of what to say. "Do you know any way I might find them?" he asked. "It might be very important."

"I'm sorry," said the man. "I don't think it's possible. All I know is that the family moved away after their daughter was in a horrible accident."

Michael suddenly felt cold. "That must be Linda Anne," he said. "Do you know what happened to her?"

"Sorry, I don't know the details," the man answered. "She had some sort of accident out in the woods. She was nearly killed. The family wanted to get far away from Phantom Valley after that."

His heart pounding, Michael thanked the man and hung up. He then told Jennifer what he'd learned.

"Whoa," she said. "You know, I think I remember hearing something about that last year. But I forgot all about it until now."

"Do you know what happened to her?" asked Michael.

"No," said Jennifer.

"Well, I hope she's not the one who has the other page," Michael said. "If she does, I'll never find it."

"Let's try the other name," suggested Jennifer. "Billy Merina." She checked for his name in the directory. "Good," she said. "A Merina family lives in Silverbell too."

Trying to remain positive, Michael punched in the new number. The phone rang six times, and he was about to hang up when a woman's voice answered. "Hello?" she said. She sounded old or sick, and for a moment Michael wondered if this woman could have a young son.

"Hello," he said. "May I speak to Billy, please?"

There was a sharp gasp as air was sucked in on the other end of the phone.

"Hello?" Michael said. "Hello?" Maybe the woman was a little deaf, he thought. "May I please speak to Billy?" he repeated loudly.

For a long moment there was no answer. Then suddenly the woman's voice came on the line again, sounding shaken. "No," she said. "You can't speak to him. Neither can anyone else. Billy's dead!"

CHAPTER 6

"**H**E'S what?" Michael cried. This time he only heard a hollow click on the other end. The woman had hung up.

"What'd she say?" Jennifer demanded. "What happened?"

Michael just stood there, the phone in his hand. He couldn't believe it. "Billy's dead," he said.

"Dead!" said Jennifer. "What happened to him?"

"I don't know," said Michael. "She just hung up."

"Wow," said Jennifer. She sank onto a bench in the hall. "This is getting really scary," she said.

"I know," said Michael, plopping down beside her. "Do you think this means that something terrible happens to everyone who gets that book?"

"Maybe not," said Jennifer. "Maybe it's just a coincidence. Maybe what happened doesn't have anything to do with the book at all."

"Maybe," said Michael. He didn't believe it, and he could tell that Jennifer didn't either. He leaned back against the wall, then sat forward quickly as something brushed his face.

Jennifer glanced at him and suddenly began screaming. "There's a huge spider on your head!" she cried.

Michael jumped up and brushed his hand across the top of his head. He felt something big and prickly. Then, to his horror, he saw a huge hairy spider fall to the floor.

"What is it?" he cried.

"I think it's a tarantula!" Jennifer jumped up on the bench.

A tarantula! Michael shuddered. "Don't worry," he said, his voice shaking. "It's more afraid of us than we are—"

"Michael, look out!" Jennifer shrieked.

Michael jumped up on the bench next to Jennifer just as the tarantula began to move toward him, its eight long, hairy legs pumping furiously.

"Go away!" he yelled at the spider. Below them, the spider, like a hairy, evil hand, stopped at the base of the bench. It seemed to look directly at Michael before starting up the leg of the bench.

"We have to kill it!" Jennifer cried.

Ordinarily Michael hated to kill anything, even insects. Now he felt he had no choice. Clenching his teeth, he kicked at the tarantula. It spun off the bench and landed on the floor. A moment later it picked itself up and ran back toward the bench. Then it started climbing again—directly toward Michael.

He could see Jennifer searching wildly for something to hit the spider with, but there was nothing. She kicked at it again. Then they both jumped off the bench, and she stomped on it. The spider lay still on the carpet for a moment. Then slowly it picked itself up. Michael could see it was injured. Only a few of its legs worked. As Michael watched in horror, the spider started toward him again, first limping, then moving faster and faster.

"Stop it!" Michael screamed. He stomped on the spider again and then again.

"I don't believe that happened!" Jennifer cried, as she stood looking at the dead tarantula.

"Me neither," said Michael. "But it did." He felt a little sick. He pulled a crumpled paper bag out of the wastebasket and picked up the spider with it, then dropped them both into the trash.

"Come on," he said. "Let's get out of here."

Once they were back in his room, Michael sank into his chair. "I've got to find that missing page," he said. "I've just got to."

"I know," agreed Jennifer.

"The only problem is there's no way to do it," he went on. He had never felt so strange in his life. Partly he was scared, but he was also confused. How could all this be happening to him?

"I just thought of something," said Jennifer suddenly. "I used to have a baby-sitter with the last name Merina. Anita Merina. It's an unusual name, and Silverbell is a small town. Maybe she's related to Billy. If so, maybe she can help us."

"It's worth trying," said Michael.

"I can get her address from my mom. Let's go into town and see her tomorrow after school."

After dinner some of the kids were having a party out on the lawn to celebrate the full moon. Usually Michael loved doing outdoor things, but now he couldn't help thinking of the animals and insects that would be out there in the dark.

If only he could somehow find a complete copy of the book. It was so old and strange that he doubted there was another copy in Silverbell. He checked in the school library just in case, but as he expected there was no *Book of the Spirits* listed in the catalog. Discouraged, he decided to stay and study for a while. He couldn't get his mind off what had happened and was still happening to him. Every time he heard a noise he checked to see if another animal or bug was after him.

A few minutes before lights-out he gave up and went back to his room. On the far side of the room Luke was already sound asleep so Michael undressed quietly.

Before getting into bed he took a few minutes to check the entire room. He peeked under the beds and in both closets. He double-checked to make sure that the door was locked and the window was shut tightly. Finally he checked under his blankets and between the sheets to make sure nothing was hiding.

There's nothing in here that can hurt me, he told himself. *Nothing at all.*

He switched off the light and crawled into bed. He was so tired that he was sure he'd fall asleep right away. But instead he couldn't get comfortable. He tried lying on his stomach, then on his side, then on his back. Finally he realized that he was too hot to sleep.

He went back to the window and opened it the slightest crack. *Nothing can get in here,* he thought. *Nothing bigger than a moth.*

He slipped back into bed, feeling the cool breeze move across his face. He had almost fallen asleep when he heard a strange, faint noise from outside. At first he thought it was sirens in the distance, but then he realized that it was howling. *Just coyotes,* he thought, relaxing. He'd heard them many times since coming to Chilleen.

He began to doze again, but the howling grew louder, and then even louder. It sounded as if the coyotes were there, at the school.

Michael was suddenly wide-awake. A moment later Luke stirred.

"Huh?" said Michael's roommate sleepily. "What's going on?"

"Coyotes," said Michael, trying to sound calm. "And I don't care how hot it is, I'm going to shut the window!"

41

As he walked over to the window, he heard Luke get out of bed behind him. "I've never heard them so loud," Luke said.

Michael pushed aside the curtain. Bright moonlight shone on the school grounds. He could see the lawn and the edge of the woods. Then he made out something else. Something dark, moving steadily toward the school.

"What's that?" cried Luke. The two boys continued to stare out the window. Now they could see that the dark shape was a small group of coyotes, three of them, maybe. The animals were beginning to trot to the school now, faster and faster, stopping every few steps to raise their heads and howl. Soon they were right under the boys' window. They could see the animals' red jaws gaping as they howled.

One of the coyotes stepped away from the others and focused directly up at Michael. He could see the animal's bloodshot eyes. A moment later it began to jump, leaping up toward the window, its sharp teeth snapping at Michael.

"Wow!" cried Luke. "Do you see that?"

Michael didn't answer. Trembling all over, he slammed the window shut.

"Hey!" said Luke. "Why'd you do that?"

"They're keeping me awake," said Michael.

"So what?" said Luke. "This is cool. I mean, I never saw coyotes so close up before." He started to open the window again.

"Don't!" Michael cried. "I mean—I've really got to get to sleep. I've got a big math test tomorrow."

"All right," said Luke with a sigh. For several minutes he remained by the window, staring down at the coyotes. Then he returned to bed.

Michael climbed into his bed, too. *Luke probably thinks I'm a wimp,* he thought. But there was no way he could tell his roommate the truth, no way Luke would believe him. Michael shut his eyes. It was no use. For many long hours he lay awake, listening to the howling coyotes as they tried to reach him. He was in terrible trouble now, he realized. The animals attacking him were getting more dangerous and bigger.

CHAPTER 7

THE next day after classes Jennifer met Michael in the dayroom. She was wearing a yellow rain poncho, and her sandy hair was already wet. "I can't believe how hard it's raining. I ran all the way here from the gym," she announced. "Did you get permission to go into Silverbell?"

Michael nodded, slipping on his raincoat.

During the whole bus ride, Michael stared out the window. He imagined he could see the eyes of the animals staring at him from the woods. Every bird in the sky seemed to be after him.

"What if Anita didn't even know Billy?" Michael asked Jennifer.

"Don't worry," she said. "I called Anita last night. My mom still had her number from when she used to baby-sit for me. Anita is Billy's cousin. When I told her I needed help with something, she promised to do anything she could. We're supposed to meet her at Billy's house."

The Merina house was two blocks from the bus stop on Elm Street. It was an old-fashioned white clapboard house with a large front porch. The front yard was overgrown with weeds, and the flower bed was bare, as if no one cared for them anymore. Jennifer rang the bell, and Michael could hear it chiming deep inside the house. A moment later a tall, pleasant-looking young woman with short brown hair opened the door.

"Anita!" said Jennifer. "How are you? This is my friend Michael."

"Good to see you, Jen," said Anita, giving the younger girl a hug. "Nice to meet you, Michael. Come on in."

They followed Anita into the dark and cluttered house. Anita took their wet coats and disappeared for a moment, coming back with a tray of sodas. "You said on the phone you needed help with something," she said to Jennifer. "What can I do for you?"

"Well, it's about Billy," said Jennifer. For a moment Anita's expression changed. She became terribly sad.

"What about him?" she said.

"We—we heard he died," Jennifer went on. "We're really sorry, Anita, even though we didn't know him. The reason we're here is we want to find out a little more about your cousin."

"I guess I don't mind talking about him," Anita said at last. "But it's a good thing Billy's mother is at work. She refuses to let anyone mention his name. It makes her too unhappy."

"How sad," said Jennifer.

"Yes, it is," said Anita. "I often come by here now to help her. Why do you want information about Billy?"

"It has to do with something that happened at Chilleen," said Michael. He gave Jennifer a meaningful glance that told her to play along with his story, and continued. "We're writing an article for the school newspaper on—on some strange things that have occurred at the school. We think Billy was connected with them in some way."

"Well, I'll do what I can to help," said Anita. "But I don't know very much about Billy's life at Chilleen. What do you want to know?"

"How long ago did he die?" asked Jennifer.

"Almost two years now," said Anita. "Sometimes it seems like yesterday."

"How did he die?" asked Jennifer. "If you don't mind telling us?"

"I guess not," said Anita. She shut her eyes a moment and frowned, the memory painful. "He was killed out in one of the canyons," she said after a moment. "Wild Horse Canyon. He was a hiker and was always going exploring. My aunt kept telling him it was dangerous to go out in the canyons alone, but Billy would never listen to her. He said he wanted to be a geologist when he grew up." For a moment it seemed as if she might cry, but then she got it together and went on. "We don't know exactly what happened, but apparently he was attacked by some sort of large animal."

"An animal!" Michael cried. He and Jennifer turned to each other nervously. "What kind of animal?" he asked.

"They never found out," said Anita. "At first they thought it was a mountain lion, but lions hardly ever attack people. Also, the medical examiner said the—the marks appeared to have been made by something much bigger. Like a giant bear."

Again Michael and Jennifer exchanged a quick glance. Michael remembered the picture in the book, the picture of the bear and its long, deadly claws.

"I know it sounds strange," said Anita, not aware of their reaction. "At first I didn't believe it myself. There are only a few bears in this part of the country, and I'd never heard of one attacking a human."

"But they never proved anything?" asked Michael.

"No," said Anita. "But then a year later, just last year, another Chilleen student was attacked in the same area. She wasn't killed, but she was badly injured."

"Did she say it was a bear?" asked Jennifer.

"She didn't remember anything about the attack," said Anita. "The doctors said it had to be a very large animal, probably a bear. But—what does all this have to do with Billy?"

"Maybe nothing," said Jennifer. "But it might be

very important. It might be a way to save another kid from being attacked the way Billy and the girl were. Was the girl named Linda Anne Rogers?"

"Why, yes," said Anita, looking surprised. "Yes, she was."

"Thanks a lot, Anita," Jennifer said. "There's just one more thing. Do you have anything of Billy's that would tell us more about him? Like—like hobbies, papers, or books?"

"Let's see," said Anita. "His big hobby was collecting and painting models of Civil War soldiers. He must have had hundreds of them. And he had several books on the Civil War, and of course all his schoolbooks."

"What happened to them?" asked Michael.

"Well," said Anita, "for months Billy's mother couldn't bear to look at them. Having them around was a reminder of his death. Finally she went into his room and cleaned it all out. There's an old man in town who collects all kinds of things. She gave the stuff to him."

"Who is the old man?" asked Michael.

"Mr. Drews, the antique dealer," Anita replied. "His shop is on Main Street across from the town square."

"Do you think he might have some of Linda Anne Rogers's things too?" asked Michael.

"It's possible," said Anita. "I remember that before her family left town they had a garage sale. They got rid of everything."

"Thanks so much," said Jennifer, giving Anita another hug.

"I was glad to do it," said Anita. "Did I help?"

Michael nodded. "Yes. More than you know."

"One of them had to have the missing page," said Jennifer as she and Michael walked up the dirt drive toward Chilleen. "Either Billy or Linda Anne."

Michael didn't answer. He was busy looking around to make sure there were no animals following him.

"Probably it's Linda Anne," Jennifer went on. "Since she had the book after Billy."

Michael saw a dark shadow moving along the side of the road. His heart began to pound faster. As he and Jennifer got closer, he saw it was just a thick bush, blowing back and forth in the wind.

"So," Jennifer went on, as if she hadn't noticed Michael's silence, "the next step is to go to Mr. Drews's store to see if he has the missing page. Then we can get the words that end the curse. What do you think?"

"Sounds good," said Michael. They had reached the front porch of the academy, and he was finally able to relax. "But how are we going to get there? I won't be able to get another pass to go into town for a few days," he added.

"I didn't think of that," Jennifer said unhappily. "I guess we'll just have to wait until the weekend to go."

The two friends shook out their raincoats and hung them on pegs in the front hall. Jennifer called her mom to come for her, and then Michael excused himself to check his mailbox. It contained one long blue envelope.

"Who's it from?" asked Jennifer.

"My dad," said Michael. He ripped the envelope open.

"What does he say?" asked Jennifer.

"My brothers were all home last weekend," Michael said, reading quickly. "They were going to have a cookout, but it got rained out. Our dachshund had puppies, and— Oh, no!"

"What's wrong?" Jennifer grabbed his arm.

"Nothing really," said Michael, crumpling the letter into a ball. "I mean, nothing I didn't expect. It's just that my dad had applied for a bank loan so I could keep coming here. Now he says the loan was turned down. So I definitely can't come back to Chilleen."

CHAPTER 8

THE next day and for most of the week it rained. Except for a few harmless mosquito bites Michael didn't have problems with animals. By Friday the beautiful spring weather was back, and he wanted to go outside again. *I won't let the curse stop me from doing what I want*, he decided.

He was excited to spend the afternoon with Duke, his favorite pony in the Chilleen stables. Riding a horse would be perfect, he thought. He'd be up high, away from any animals that might try to attack him from the ground.

He looked carefully around before going out the back door to the stables. Just when he decided the coast was clear, he heard someone grunting behind him. He turned around and saw Mr. Grady wearing a big backpack.

"Hello, Mr. Grady," he said.

"Good afternoon," the cook answered. "You're Chub's friend, aren't you?"

"Yes," said Michael, remembering Chubber's strange friendship with the cook. "I'm Michael."

"Looks like a good day for the outdoors," Mr. Grady went on.

"Are you going hiking?" asked Michael.

"You might say that," said Mr. Grady. "There are some things out in the mountains that I'm very interested in." He waved, then started walking toward the teachers' parking lot.

That guy is too weird, thought Michael. *He's obviously out of shape—so how come he keeps going hiking?*

By the time he got to the stable he had forgotten about the cook. The old building was empty. Vern, the stableman, wasn't around. He went into the tack room and selected a saddle. Then he walked back into the main stable and headed toward Duke's stall. As he walked through the stables he heard the horses whinnying nervously, as if they were afraid of something. He saw nothing strange, nothing that didn't belong.

The big black and white pony was standing calmly in his stall as Michael approached. He was reaching out to open the door to the stall when Duke whipped his head around and stared Michael right in the eye. A moment later the horse began whinnying and pawing the ground and knocking against the door.

Startled, Michael jumped out of the way. What could

have gotten into Duke? Nervously he peeked around the stable, but saw nothing that shouldn't be there. Again he reached for the door of the stall. Duke acted more upset than ever, rising up on his back hooves and pawing the air twice.

"What is it, Duke?" he asked calmly. "What is it, boy?"

The horse lowered his hooves and thrust out its head and snapped at Michael's arm. Michael pulled back in time, but dropped the saddle.

It's me! he realized, horrified. *Duke is upset by me! He's trying to attack me!*

"It's only me, Duke boy," he said. But the pony continued to buck and whinny.

"Okay, okay," Michael said. He picked up the saddle and started back for the tack room. As he walked past the other stalls, the horses in them began to whinny and kick the boards.

The noise grew louder. The horses began to hit the rough wood planks harder and faster.

Crash! Crash!

Michael heard the sound of splintering wood. The horses' eyes were wild, their muzzles flecked with foam. All of them were knocking against their stalls now. In a minute they'd break out. Then they'd come after him with their hooves and teeth.

"No!" Michael cried. "No!" He dropped the saddle on the floor and ran out of the stable, slamming the door behind him. He kept running across the corral, trying to get as far from the screaming horses as he could.

On the far side of the corral he stopped, out of breath, and leaned against the fence. His heart was pounding as if he'd just run a race. *Before, it was just strange animals,* he thought. *I could stay away from them. But now even the animals I know are after me. The danger is all around me now.*

"Duke *attacked* you?" For a moment Jennifer acted as if she didn't believe Michael. It was Saturday afternoon and Michael had gotten permission to go to Silverbell. While they waited for the bus, Michael told her what had happened the day before.

"Just like your cat attacked me," Michael said. "I'm not safe from anything now."

"Wow," said Jennifer.

When the bus pulled up, they boarded it and moved to the back. Just as they were sitting down, Mr. Grady came running up to the bus stop, panting. He got on the bus and stopped a minute to catch his breath, then sat in the seat behind the driver.

"He's always running around," Michael said, pointing at Mr. Grady. "Yesterday he went out hiking, if you can believe it."

Jennifer shrugged. "Maybe he's trying to get in shape," she said. "Anyway, what happened after Duke attacked you?"

"Nothing much," said Michael. "Like I told you, I got away."

Jennifer shook her head, then turned to look out the bus window. "Well, let's just hope we can find that missing page in Mr. Drews's shop," she said. "The sooner we end this curse, the better."

Michael didn't answer. He was thinking about what had happened the day before at the stable. Plus, it didn't seem likely to him that Mr. Drews would have the page that had been torn out of his textbook. If he didn't, where else could Michael find the words to end the curse? Would he have to spend the rest of his life watching out for animals? Nobody could live that way.

"Michael?" said Jennifer. "Are you okay?"

"Fine," he said. "I was just thinking about something."

"How should we do this?" she went on. "Should we just tell Mr. Drews what we want?"

"I guess so," said Michael. "I mean, it's not like we want to take anything. We just want to look for that piece of paper."

Mr. Drews's shop was on Main Street two doors down from the ice-cream parlor. The antique store was in an old house converted into a shop. Michael noticed that it hadn't been painted in a long time.

"Drews's Antiques," Jennifer read the faded brown sign over the door.

The two windows on either side of the door were jammed with dusty objects of every sort. A quick glance showed Michael old clothing, furniture, dishes, books, and paintings.

"Anything could be in there," Jennifer said.

When they opened the door, they heard a bell ring in the back. Inside, the shop was even more crowded than it had looked from the outside. The entire place was crammed with things. Even the ceiling was crowded with dozens of hanging lamps, mobiles, and model airplanes.

"I wonder how anyone finds anything in this place," Michael said out loud.

There was a noise from the back of the shop, and a moment later a stooped-over old white-haired man with a long mustache appeared from the back of the store.

"What do you want?" the old man shouted. He looked suspicious and mean.

"Why, we're—uh—just looking," Jennifer said quickly. She leaned over and pretended to examine an antique doll in a pink dress.

"What did you say?" Mr. Drews cupped a hand around his ear, and Michael realized he was hard of hearing.

"She said she was just looking!" Michael shouted back. He realized there was no use telling Mr. Drews what they wanted.

"Make it snappy," shouted the old man. He looked at Michael suspiciously.

Feeling nervous, Michael began to look around, hoping to find any sign that Billy's or Linda Anne's things were here. But the store was so crowded he realized it could take hours to find anything. He walked farther back in the store, along a narrow aisle made by stacking furniture pieces one on top of the other. Mr. Drews followed him with his eyes.

"This isn't a museum," the old man said after a moment. "Are you looking for anything specific?"

"Yes," answered Jennifer quickly. She faced him and began talking loudly. "We're working on a school play about life at the Chilleen Academy," she said. "We were wondering if you had any old things that belonged to Chilleen students in the past. We—uh—want to buy them to use as props."

Michael rolled his eyes. What a stupid story, he thought.

The old man continued to stare at Jennifer, his face more suspicious than ever. "Why would I have things belonging to former Chilleen students?" he said at last.

"We thought you might have bought some at a yard sale or something," said Michael quickly. "This is really the only secondhand store in Silverbell."

"Well, look around, then," said Mr. Drews. "Everything's all mixed together. And I don't have all day." He checked his watch.

Michael and Jennifer took different sides of the shop and began to search. Michael became discouraged by the nearly hopeless job. He'd never seen so many different things lying on shelves and tables, jumbled together in boxes, stacked in corners. There was a big bookshelf crammed with books, and Michael began to search through it for *Book of the Spirits*. On the bottom shelf he saw an old dusty book. Through the dust on the cover he could just make out the word *Spirits*. Excited, he pulled out the book and dusted it off, revealing the full title: *Spirits of the Night*. Disappointed, he shoved it back and then began sneezing.

He was about to continue his search on a nearby table when Mr. Drews cleared his throat. "I got to close up for a while," he told Michael and Jennifer. "You two get on out now."

"But—" Michael started to say.

"I mean it!" the old man said. "I've got an important business appointment. You can come back another day."

"Come on, Jennifer," Michael said. The old man kept his eyes glued to Jennifer and Michael as they started to leave.

It's no use, Michael thought. *Even if he has the things, we could never find them in a million years.*

On the way out the door he suddenly saw a shelf he hadn't noticed before. On one half of the shelf were piled familiar-looking books. He glanced at the spines. *Fundamental Geometry*, said one book. The other was called *History for Middle-School Students*.

He recognized the books. They were the same ones he and his friends used at Chilleen. Next to the books was a mass of tiny figures. Michael realized they were toy soldiers. Each tiny figure had been carefully painted in gray or blue. They were soldiers of the Civil War, the kind Anita told them Billy had collected.

He reached out to check what else was in the pile of books, but Mr. Drews was shouting again. At the same time, so loud it blocked out the old man's voice, there was another noise, a roaring. The sound was so loud and so familiar that Michael felt as if his heart had stopped. It was the same noise he had heard when he read the curse, the same roaring he'd heard in the cave.

CHAPTER 9

THE roaring grew even louder. Michael felt it was trying to tell him something. Then, as suddenly as it had started, the roaring faded away.

Michael was standing there a moment, wondering what to do, when Mr. Drews began shouting again. "I said get out of here!" the old man yelled. With a last look at the toy soldiers, Michael followed Jennifer out the door.

"Did you hear something strange in there?" he asked when they were on the sidewalk.

"The only strange thing I heard was Mr. Drews yelling," grumbled Jennifer.

"You didn't hear a roaring noise?" Michael went on.

"No," said Jennifer. "Why?"

"Nothing," replied Michael. They began to walk down

the board sidewalk toward the town square. After a moment Michael said, "I saw a whole shelf with toy soldiers and schoolbooks. They might have been Billy's."

"I saw some dolls," said Jennifer. "I was wondering if they could be Linda Anne's."

"I've got to find a way to check out those things," Michael declared.

"We'll think of something," said Jennifer. The next bus back to the school wasn't for an hour, so they wandered across to the town square and the displays of western crafts.

As Michael was examining some polished stones, a shadow fell across his face. He raised his eyes to a large hawk circling directly above him. With each completed circle the bird dropped a little lower. Michael felt like the bull's-eye on a target.

"Come on," he said quickly to Jennifer. "Let's go inside. Let's—uh, get an ice cream."

The Silverbell Emporium was nearly empty. Jennifer and Michael had their pick of seats in the row of booths lining the wall. Jennifer chose the booth farthest away from the front door. "I like it back here," she said. "No one can see us. It's like our own private ice-cream place." She scrunched down even more in the old-fashioned high-backed wooden seat.

The waitress brought their orders, hot fudge sundaes, and they both dug in. For a moment Michael felt almost normal, as if he weren't being chased by all the animals in Phantom Valley.

"I just wish I knew what Mr. Drews really has in his store," Michael said, licking fudge off his thumb. "I wish there was some way to—"

"I tell you I won't sell it!" came a voice from the next booth. Michael and Jennifer stared at each other in surprise. Someone else must have come in while they were ordering.

"That sounds like Mr. Drews," Jennifer said, her finger to her lips.

"I know," whispered Michael. The back of the booth was too high to see over, but they could hear all right. Whoever was in the booth with Mr. Drews was speaking very quietly, maybe even whispering. Mr. Drews's loud, hoarse voice could be made out clearly.

"Because I've spent too much time looking for it!" Mr. Drews's voice boomed. "I finally found it in some kid's old junk. Besides, I've decided to sell it, and the price is much higher than you're offering!"

"Who's he talking to?" Jennifer whispered.

Michael pushed his ear against the back of the booth, but the other voice was only a soft whisper.

"I guess it's just business," said Michael after a moment. "We probably shouldn't be listening anyway."

"We can't help it," said Jennifer. "His voice is so loud."

For the next few minutes Mr. Drews and the person he was with continued to talk, but more quietly. Michael was just finishing up the syrup at the bottom of his sundae glass when Mr. Drews's voice boomed out again.

"Of course I'm sure!" he yelled. Michael and Jennifer burst into giggles. They became instantly more serious when they heard his next words. "It's just the way the legends described it," Mr. Drews went on. "The bear, the claws, every detail fits. Every book on Phantom Valley has the same story, and it matches exactly."

Michael and Jennifer were very interested now.

The other person whispered something to Mr. Drews, and Mr. Drews answered angrily. "Because it's the most important find in Phantom Valley in years, that's why! It goes to the highest bidder! So you're wasting your time!" He suddenly stood up, and Jennifer and Michael both turned quickly, scrunching even farther down in their seats so no one could see them. All they needed was for Mr. Drews to think they'd been spying on him.

The other person with Mr. Drews got up too. "We'll see about that," he said in a familiar voice. "Perhaps you'll change your mind."

Then both men walked out of the Emporium. Michael poked his head out from the booth to see if he recognized the man with Mr. Drews, but he'd already left the shop.

"Did you hear that?" asked Jennifer.

"You bet I did," said Michael. "And I'll tell you one thing. No matter what he was talking about, if it has to do with legends and bears, I'm going to find out about it."

"But how?" said Jennifer. "We can't let Mr. Drews know we were spying on him."

"We weren't spying," answered Michael. "Is it our fault he talks so loud?"

By the time they got back to Chilleen, Jennifer and Michael had decided to see if they could find more information on the legends Mr. Drews had mentioned. "I'll bet there's a ton of books on the legends of the Old West in the school library," said Michael. "Maybe one of them even tells how to end the curse."

They climbed the stairs and headed into the library. According to the computer catalog, there were half a dozen books on the legends of Phantom Valley. Michael carefully copied the names and reference numbers, then followed Jennifer into the stacks where those books were kept.

"I'm positive we'll find the answer here," Jennifer said. "I'm just sure of it."

They found the numbers they wanted, but not one of the books was on the shelf. "I don't believe this!" cried Michael after a moment. "They're all gone!"

"Maybe they're in the locked stacks," said Jennifer. "Let's ask at the desk."

Ms. Martin, the librarian, lifted her head from some notes. "Yes?" she said with a pleasant smile.

"We're looking for these books," said Jennifer, holding out the slip Michael had written. "But none of them seems to be in the stacks."

"Just a moment," said Ms. Martin. "Let me check." She ran her fingers over the keyboard of her computer and squinted at the screen. "I'm sorry," she said after a moment. "But all those books are checked out."

"All of them!" cried Michael.

"Yes," she said. "They were all checked out on the same day last week."

"Who has them?" asked Jennifer.

"I'm sorry," said the librarian. "I can't let you have that information."

"But I have to see those books!" said Michael. "It's important."

"I'm sure it is," said Ms. Martin. "But I'm afraid there's nothing I can do. They're due back in just a few days. Why don't you check back here next week?"

Sure, Michael thought. *I can do that. If I'm still alive next week.*

CHAPTER 10

MONDAY morning was cool, and Michael pulled his jacket tight as he crossed the back lawn to the classroom annex. As always when he was outside, he kept his eyes open, scanning the area for animals, bugs, and birds. He jumped as something flew past him on the lawn, then relaxed. It was just a Frisbee, thrown by one of the James twins.

When he got to his first class, science lab, he was glad to see that the windows were closed. He had come early so he could check out the room. He peered under all the desks and in the cupboards, and there were no insects or animals hiding. *I'll be safe at least for the next hour,* he thought.

"Good morning, class," said Mr. Rothrock a few minutes later. Next to the teacher was a tall, red-haired woman carrying a big cardboard box. "I have a surprise for you," Mr. Rothrock went on. "This is Dr. Teitle from the junior college. She's an expert on reptiles. She's agreed to show us one of her prize snakes."

Everyone cheered at the break from regular class. Dr. Teitle put her box down on Mr. Rothrock's desk and began telling the class all about snakes. "Even though they are deadly hunters," she said, "most snakes are harmless to humans. Not all snakes kill their prey by biting. Some snakes crush their victims to death. They wrap themselves tightly around the bodies of the victims."

She opened the box and reached in, then brought out a yellow- and white-striped snake. "This is a corn snake," she told the class. "It's completely harmless—to us. But it can be deadly to any animal it decides to attack."

"Would someone like to help Dr. Teitle with the snake?" asked Mr. Rothrock. "Michael, what about you?"

Michael felt as if his heart had stopped.

"No, I really don't feel like it," he said, focusing on the floor.

"Come on, Michael. Give Dr. Teitle a hand. She said the snake was harmless," Mr. Rothrock said, gesturing for Michael to come to the front of the class.

"I—I—" he stammered. What was he going to say? *No, Mr. Rothrock, I can't, the snake might attack me.*

"Hey, Michael's afraid of the snake," Randy Moser announced, laughing. This made a bunch of other kids in the class laugh too. Michael could feel his face turn red. Mr. Rothrock was staring at him.

"Um—all right," he said. He didn't seem to have a choice.

It's just a harmless snake, he told himself as he walked up to the front of the room.

"Many people think snakes are cold and slimy," said Dr. Teitle. She held the snake out to Michael. "What does it feel like to you?"

Michael touched the snake. "It's warm," he said. "Warm and soft."

The snake met Michael's gaze, then began to slither up his arm.

"Oh, it likes you," said Dr. Teitle. Everyone in the class laughed.

The snake began to wind itself around Michael's arm. Dr. Teitle turned to the blackboard and drew a picture of a snake. "Snakes are different from most other animals," she said. "For instance, many snakes have only one lung and one kidney."

The snake tightened itself around Michael's arm. Then it let go and slithered onto his shoulder. Slowly it began to coil itself around his neck. Michael put his hands up to pull the snake away. The animal was strong. Every time he managed to pull part of it away from his neck, another part wrapped itself back around him. Some of the kids began to laugh. Michael realized that they thought he was clowning around.

"Most snakes don't need to eat as often as other animals," Dr. Teitle said. "In fact, some of the bigger snakes sometimes eat only every month or two."

The snake wound itself even tighter around Michael's throat. *It's choking me!* he realized. Using both hands, he tried to pull it away, but the snake coiled tighter, tighter. Spots began to appear before Michael's eyes. He could barely hear the kids in the class laughing now. He knew that they still thought he was goofing.

He tried to cry for help, but didn't have enough breath. He grew weaker. *No,* he thought in horror. *No, no . . .* Just as he was about to black out, Dr. Teitle turned around to see why everyone was laughing. "For heaven's sake!" she said. Quickly she ran over to Michael and tugged at the snake. It took all her strength to pull the snake off Michael.

He staggered against Mr. Rothrock's desk, gulping in lungfuls of air. "Are you all right?" she asked Michael. Weakly, he nodded. "I just don't understand it," she said. "I've never seen a corn snake act that way before."

Michael stood up and tried a weak grin. "I guess it's like you said," he told her hoarsely. "I guess it just likes me."

Everyone laughed, but he knew the opposite of what he'd said was true. He knew that the snake, like all the animals in Phantom Valley, hated him. Hated him enough to try to kill him.

After biology class Michael had study hall, which was in the library in the main building. He was still embarrassed and upset about what had happened with the snake.

As he was crossing the lawn back to the main building, he heard a sudden noise. Just above him, perched among the branches of an oak tree, was a huge raven. The bird was staring directly at him.

Keeping his eye on the bird, Michael began to walk more quickly toward the back door of the academy. The raven rustled its wings. Michael broke into a run.

He had nearly reached the door when the bird flew into the air and swooped down toward him. His heart pounding in his chest, Michael fell against the door, pushing it open. He rolled inside and shut the door as quickly as he could. Then he sat there a moment, breathing heavily.

"Why, Michael, whatever is the matter?" Michael saw Mr. Elias, the dean of boys, standing above him, surprise on his face.

"Nothing," Michael said. "I was—uh—practicing *t'ai chi,* and I tripped and fell against the door."

"You're lucky you weren't hurt," said the administrator, offering Michael a hand up. "I suggest you try to be more careful from now on."

"I promise," said Michael. Deep inside, he knew that no matter how careful he was it wouldn't do any good unless he could somehow get rid of the curse.

Michael was inside a cool, damp cave. The air inside the cave echoed with the strange roaring noise, the noise he had heard before. Standing against the back wall was a huge black bear. On each of its paws was one long, sharp claw. The bear threw back its head and roared. Then there was a bright flash of light, and the bear vanished.

Where the bear had been standing there was now only a golden yellow glow. Michael felt drawn to the glow. As if hypnotized, he slowly walked toward it. As he got closer he could see that the glow was coming from a niche in the wall of the cave. The niche was the shape and size of a shoe box. There was something very familiar about it. . . .

Michael awoke with a start. He looked around, half expecting to see the cave and the little nook. Then he realized he'd been dreaming. It had seemed so real. The cave, the bear, the niche . . . Suddenly he remembered where he'd seen the niche before. It was the same one he'd seen in the back of the cave that day with Chubber!

Why would he dream about that cave? And why was the bear with one claw on each paw in the dream?

He was still trying to figure out what the dream meant when the door to his room flew open and Luke came running in.

"Hey, roomie," Luke said. "I thought you'd never wake up. Are you ready for the field trip?"

"What field trip?" said Michael, sitting up in bed. And then he remembered. He'd signed up for a history field trip to Aramaca Canyon. "I don't think I'm going," he said to Luke. "I have a sore throat this morning."

"Don't be a wimp," said Luke. "Everyone's going. Come on. The fresh air will make you feel better."

For a moment Michael considered going. He imagined the pale morning sun reflected on the red walls of the canyon and the clear blue sky above. Then he imagined something else: insects, birds, and animals, all after him. Even if he didn't have to worry about an attack, how could he go ride when he couldn't even get near his pony?

"No," he repeated. "Thanks anyway. I just don't feel right."

Luke gave him a funny look, then grinned again. "Whatever you say," he said. "In that case, can I borrow your leather jacket?"

"Sure," said Michael. "It's on the back of the chair over there."

"Thanks," said Luke. "See you tonight." He ran out of the room.

Michael pulled on his jeans, thinking about the field trip. If only he could go riding and hiking the way he used to. *Maybe I'll feel better if I shoot some baskets over at the gym,* he thought. And then he remembered that the key to his locker was in his leather jacket.

Michael jumped to his feet and ran out the door and down the stairs. He had to catch Luke before the ride started. He ran across the lawn and around to the back and through the woods toward the stables. Across the broad field in front of the stables he could see Luke in his jacket. He was running up to the corral.

Then, without warning there was a faint growling noise and a dark form shot out of the stable and knocked Luke down. Michael froze. It was Rex, the stable dog.

He heard Luke scream as he tried to fight the dog off. Michael could see his friend's fists pounding the dog, his legs kicking it. He could hear the growls all the way across the field. It looked as if the dog was trying to kill Luke.

I've got to help Luke, Michael thought. He was afraid, but he ignored his fear and took off across the field to help his roommate. A moment later a man in a gray shirt came running out of the stables. Michael recognized Vern, the stableman. In one quick movement Vern pulled the growling dog off Luke and snapped a leash on Rex's collar.

He was helping Luke stand up when Michael reached them.

"Are you sure you're all right, boy?" Vern asked, sounding worried. Beside him, Rex pulled at his leash, growling and snarling.

"I'm fine," said Luke. "For some reason, the dog only bit the jacket."

"Luke!" Michael cried.

"Hi, Michael," said Luke, his face very pale beneath his freckles.

"Are you all right? I saw the dog attack you."

"I'm all right," said Luke. "But your jacket isn't so great." He held up his arm. The leather sleeve of the jacket hung down in tattered shreds.

"I don't know what's gotten into this dog," said Vern, obviously worried. "He's usually gentle as a lamb."

"Probably he just thought Luke was someone else," said Michael. "Like an intruder."

"Maybe so," said Vern, leading the dog off. "But I'm going to have him checked out by the vet."

"I'm really sorry about your jacket," Luke told Michael.

"It's okay," said Michael. "But that's why I'm out here. I remembered that I need my jacket today after all."

"Why?" said Luke. "You aren't going on the field trip."

"I still need it," Michael said. He realized how lame he sounded. How could he tell Luke that wearing the jacket outdoors could put Luke in terrible danger? "I'm sorry," said Michael. "Just let me have it."

"Sure," said Luke, suddenly angry. "It's all ripped now anyway." He pulled off the jacket and tossed it to Michael. Then he ran off to the stables.

Sadly, Michael watched him go. Rex had thought Luke was someone else, all right, he realized. The dog hadn't thought Luke was an intruder. No, he'd caught the scent on Michael's jacket. Michael's scent. Those ugly tooth marks had been meant for him.

CHAPTER 11

"**H**OW'S your work study going?" Chubber asked Michael. The two boys had just finished studying together in the library and were making their way down the stairs to the dayroom.

"Not bad," said Michael. His job was working in the administration office two mornings a week.

"I've been working in the dining room," said Chubber. "But I'm going to try to get transferred to the kitchen."

"Right," said Michael. "So you can get free eats any time you want."

Chubber seemed to be embarrassed. "No," he said. "It's because I think Mr. Grady needs help. I'm positive he's never cooked before."

"His food sure is bad," said Michael. "Why would he take a job as a cook if he isn't one?"

"I don't know," said Chubber. "But I figure I can help. Hey, speaking of Mr. Grady—" He pointed out a front hall window to the porch, where Mr. Grady was sitting on the swing. There was a big pile of books next to him.

"I wonder what he's studying?" Michael asked.

"Cooking, I hope," said Chubber. He moved closer to the window. "I can almost see what he's reading," he whispered, squinting out the window. "Hey, that's weird—he's looking at a picture of a big bear."

"Really?" said Michael, instantly interested.

"Yeah," said his friend. "It's a strange-looking bear, though. It's got only one claw on each paw."

It sounded just like the picture of the bear on the page with the curse. "I want to see something in that book," Michael said. "Could you do me a favor and distract Mr. Grady for a minute?"

"What do you mean?"

"Just do something to get him away for a couple of minutes. I want to look in his book."

"Why don't you just ask him to see it?"

For a moment Michael considered doing just that. But something about Mr. Grady made him nervous. Anyway, the fewer people who knew about the trouble he was in, the better. "Just do it, okay?" he repeated.

"Okay," said Chub, puzzled. Then he smiled. "Actually, you just gave me an idea." The boys stepped out on the porch. Then all innocence, Chubber walked up to Mr. Grady. "Excuse me, sir," he said. "I was wondering if you'd let me into the kitchen for a snack. I don't think I can hold out till dinner."

"Just a minute," said Mr. Grady. He finished reading, then marked his place with a postcard and got up out of the swing. "I know how you feel," he said with a wink. "I could use a slice of pie myself. Would your friend like to join us?"

"No, thanks," said Michael. "I'll wait here."

Chubber followed Mr. Grady inside. Michael checked around the porch carefully to make sure there were no animals or insects hiding. Then he sat down on the swing. When he looked closely at the pile of books, his heart began racing. These were the exact books he and Jennifer had been looking for on Saturday night! Mr. Grady was the one who had checked out all the books on the legends of Phantom Valley.

Quickly he opened the one Mr. Grady had been reading. It was a heavy book bound in red leather. The title, *Ghost Animals of Phantom Valley*, was printed on the spine in gold letters.

Michael turned to the page Mr. Grady had marked. The chapter was titled "The Great Bear." Michael began to read.

One of the oldest legends tells of a band of early men who came to the valley. They carried with them statues of their holy animals. It is said that they hid their most important statue—one of a bear—in a nook in a secret cave.

The statue is said to be protected by a curse. The curse will begin working if the bear is ever removed from the cave. Anyone who then says the words of the curse will fall under its spell. The curse brings misfortune and death. It can be removed only by doing two things. First, the bear statue must be returned to its resting place. Then, the person under the curse must repeat the sacred words.

There are many stories about the famous bear idol, which has never been found.

Bear idol! Michael could hardly believe his eyes. He peered again at the picture he and Chubber had seen through the front window. There was no doubt it was the same bear on the odd page in his textbook. Every detail was the same, from the sharp teeth to the deadly single claw on each paw.

He continued to stare at the drawing, his heart racing. Now he understood how he had caused the curse to work. More important, he knew he had to do *two* things to end it. He had to find the sacred words on the missing page, and he had to find and return the bear statue to its cave.

How could he do it? He didn't even know where the bear idol was.

The roaring noise rose unexpectedly in his ears just then, and he had a vision of the cave from his dream. The cave! The cave that he and Chubber had found while they were out hiking. They were the same. Michael felt the hair on the back of his neck stand up.

Somehow he *knew* the cave he'd found was the cave in the bear legend—the cave where the bear statue had been hidden all those years ago.

Michael then realized what he had to do. He had to go back to the cave, to see if he could find the bear statue. Maybe over the years it had fallen out of its shrine, and all he had to do was pick it up and put it back. Or, if it wasn't in the cave, maybe he'd find a clue to where it was now.

He was so absorbed that he'd forgotten all about Mr. Grady until a large shadow fell across the page. He looked up to see the cook, staring down at him, with a strange expression on his face.

"I was just looking at your book," Michael said nervously. "It's really interesting."

Mr. Grady continued to stare at him. "Yes, it is," he said after a moment. Then he added, "More interesting than you know."

That night Michael called Jennifer and told her what he had found out.

"You're kidding!" she said. "You mean the curse has to do with a statue?"

"It looks like it," said Michael, and then he told her about his dream. "I've already gotten permission to go hiking tomorrow," he said. "So I'll go to the cave after school. After that dream, I'm sure it's the same cave as the one in the legend."

"But, Michael," protested Jennifer, "you said you need to do two things to end the curse. Even if you manage to find the bear and put it back, you don't know the words."

"Maybe they're written on the bear," said Michael. "I don't know. All I know is I have to try."

Jennifer was silent for a moment. "I'll go with you," she said. "It's too dangerous for you to be outside alone, with all the animals after you."

"I can't let you," said Michael. "It could be dangerous for you, too."

"The animals aren't after me," she said. "If anything tries to attack you, I'll just shoo it away. I won't take no for an answer," she went on. "I'll meet you tomorrow at the bike rack ten minutes after classes are over."

The next day was cloudy and Michael was afraid it would rain and spoil his plan. By afternoon the sun had come out, and he raced to his bicycle to meet Jennifer. She was wearing her day pack and a canteen on her belt, and she had an aluminum baseball bat strapped to the frame of her bike. When he saw it, Michael almost laughed. "What's that for?" he said.

"Protection," said Jennifer. "If anything tries to attack you, we can scare it away with the bat."

The two friends rode as quickly as they could and soon were at Wild Horse Canyon. They left their bicycles at the base of the cliffs and began climbing the steep, rocky trail. Jennifer carried the baseball bat with her.

Except for a few insects and one ground squirrel that he chased away with a rock, no animals attacked him on the climb. *Maybe the curse is getting weaker*, Michael thought.

The cave was much darker than it had been when he and Chub had visited in the morning. Michael had to switch on his flashlight.

"Wow," said Jennifer. "What a spooky place!"

Together the two friends began exploring every inch of the cave. Except for rocks and a few dried leaves that had been blown in, it seemed to be completely empty.

When they got to the back of the cave, Michael braced himself. Would he hear the awful roaring sound again?

He showed Jennifer the niche he had found in the wall. He reached out to touch it. *Roar!*

Michael glanced at Jennifer. "Did you hear that?" he asked.

"Hear what?" said Jennifer.

The hollow roar came again. Then it faded. Michael shook his head.

Jennifer ran her hand along the inside of the niche. "It's so smooth," she said. "It must be man-made."

"I know," said Michael. "This has to be the shrine. Maybe the statue of the bear somehow fell out of it and is buried in the floor."

They squatted down and ran their hands along the hard, smooth rock floor. There were no bumps that didn't seem to belong, or any soft spots where something might have worked its way into the dirt. Michael took out his pocketknife and tried to dig into the floor of the cave, but the blade of his knife bent.

"I don't see how anything could be buried here," said Jennifer. "The rock's too hard. Someone must have taken the bear out of the cave."

"I guess so," said Michael, sitting with his back against the cave wall. Even though he had known the chances of finding the bear statue were slim, he felt very disappointed. "If that's true, then it could have been taken any time in the last few centuries. The idol could be anywhere now."

"I know," said Jennifer. "Maybe it's still somewhere in Phantom Valley. At least we have to try to find it here."

"Maybe," said Michael. Then he had a sudden idea. "This is a long shot, but maybe it's in Mr. Drews's antique store."

"Maybe that's what he was talking about with that man in the soda shop the other day. Remember? He talked about something he had that was really valuable," Jennifer said, excited.

"You're right," agreed Michael. He remembered how Mr. Drews had said it was the most valuable thing ever found in Phantom Valley. "But if Mr. Drews has it," he went on, "where would it be? He wouldn't just keep it out on a shelf in his shop."

"Probably not," said Jennifer. "But if he has the

bear, maybe he also has the page with the words for ending the curse. We've got to go back to the shop to see what we can find."

"We've got to give it a try at least. It's my only option," said Michael. "I just wonder if—" His words were cut off by a sudden snarling sound. At first he thought it was the roaring again.

"What's that?" asked Jennifer, sounding startled.

"Did you hear it too?" asked Michael. He realized the snarling was coming from *outside* the cave. And it was moving closer to them.

A shadow slid across the front of the cave.

"What is—" Jennifer started to say.

"Sh!" hissed Michael. "Be quiet. Maybe whatever it is will go away."

They sat still, scarcely breathing. "Michael!" Jennifer shrieked all at once. "It's—oh, no!"

Michael looked toward the front of the cave. Padding quietly through the entrance was a large tawny mountain lion.

CHAPTER 12

JENNIFER screamed again.

Michael, paralyzed with fear, just stared at the big cat. The mountain lion took another step into the cave. Its nose was quivering as it picked up their scent. Michael watched its sharp white teeth as the animal snarled, its lips pulled back.

One of the most deadly of all animals was now after Michael.

He picked up the aluminum baseball bat and held it out in front of him. He didn't have much hope that he could hurt the cat, but maybe he could scare it away.

The lion took another step closer to them and opened its mouth to growl again. Then it stopped and focused in on Michael.

His arms shaking, Michael swung the baseball bat at

the cat. It snarled again and went into a crouch. Its tail twitched, and Michael realized that it was getting ready to spring.

He shut his eyes, terrified.

Boom!

A shot rang out outside the cave and sounded over and over again inside. The noise of the shot was followed by an angry snarl. Michael opened his eyes just in time to see the mountain lion run out of the cave.

"What happened?" Jennifer cried.

"I don't know," said Michael. "I—"

"You kids all right?" Michael raised his head in surprise. Mr. Grady was standing in the entrance to the cave with a shotgun in his hand.

"Mr. Grady!" Jennifer said. "What are you doing here?"

He didn't answer. "It's lucky I was hiking nearby," he said.

"Did you hurt the mountain lion?" asked Michael, suddenly feeling guilty.

"Nah," said the big man. "Just scared it away."

Michael got shakily to his feet. This was the second time he and Mr. Grady had both been at the cave at the same time. He didn't think it was an accident. "Were you following us?" he asked Mr. Grady, only half joking.

"Now, why would you think a thing like that?" asked Mr. Grady.

Because it's true, Michael thought. He thought again

about Mr. Grady—how he was pretending to be a cook, why he was reading all those books on Phantom Valley, and now why he had shown up at the cave again. "You're not really a cook, are you?" Michael said suddenly.

"Michael!" said Jennifer, shocked.

"It's okay," the big man said. "I don't mind answering. No, I'm not a cook. How'd you know?"

"For one thing, I've been eating your food," said Michael.

Instead of being insulted, Mr. Grady laughed. "Well, I did my best," he said.

"If you're not a cook," said Jennifer, "then what are you doing at the Chilleen Academy?"

"The school is near Wild Horse Canyon," answered Mr. Grady. "You see, I'm an archeologist. I collect things for museums."

"For real?" said Jennifer. "You mean like Indiana Jones?"

"A little like that," said Mr. Grady, laughing again.

"What museum?" said Michael.

"I work for several museums," said Mr. Grady vaguely. "Some of the most important ones in the country."

"Is that why you're here?" asked Jennifer. "To get something for one of your museums?"

"That's right," said Mr. Grady. "One of my clients heard about an ancient animal statue that a kid found around here a couple of years ago. They sent me here to see if I could find it."

Michael just stared at Mr. Grady. "Was the statue of a bear?" he asked suspiciously.

"Why, yes, it was," said Mr. Grady. "How do you know about the bear?"

"We read about it," said Michael quickly. "In some old books on Phantom Valley."

"Then you know how valuable it is," said Mr. Grady. "How valuable it would be to any museum."

Not to mention to my life, Michael thought, but he didn't say anything. In the first place, he wasn't sure Mr. Grady would believe him. In the second place, he didn't trust Mr. Grady. Why should he? Mr. Grady had lied about being a cook, and he was probably lying about being an archeologist. Why would any archeologist have to pretend to be a cook?

"I hope you find the bear," said Jennifer.

"Oh, I've already found it," said Mr. Grady. "That is, I know who has it. But unfortunately the man who has it wants to sell it to a rich collector in Europe."

"That's terrible," said Jennifer.

"I agree," said Mr. Grady. "But I'm afraid my museum can't afford to pay as much as the collector."

"So the statue's going to end up in Europe?" Michael asked, suddenly fearful.

"It looks that way," Mr. Grady said evasively. "I've only got until tomorrow—"

"Tomorrow?" said Michael. "What's happening tomorrow?"

Mr. Grady looked uncomfortable. "Well," he began, "the man who has it is planning to ship it off then."

Tomorrow! Michael felt a sudden cold chill. If Mr. Drews sent the statue to Europe the next day, Michael would never be able to end the curse. "Is the man who has it Mr. Drews at the antique store?" Michael asked.

"I must say you two seem to know a great deal about the statue," Mr. Grady said suspiciously. "Did Drews tell you he had it?" he asked.

"No," said Michael. "But we know he has a lot of old things in his store, so we just thought he might be the one."

Mr. Grady fell silent for a moment, deep in thought. "You're right. Drews has it," he said finally. "But he's not going to have it much longer. If you two know what's good for you, you'll forget all about the bear. Forget you ever heard of it. Understand?"

Mr. Grady's voice was cold and held the promise of a threat. For a moment Michael was afraid. "Yes, sir," he said. "Come on, Jennifer."

"But, Michael—" she started to say as he grabbed her hand and dragged her out of the cave.

"Come *on*."

"So Mr. Drews *does* have the bear," said Jennifer as they rode into Silverbell. "I wonder if he also knows the words to end the curse."

"I don't know, but we have to get the statue from him," said Michael. "The problem is how."

"Why did you make me shut up back there in the cave?"

"I don't trust Mr. Grady," he answered.

"I just wanted to find out more about the bear," Jennifer said, sounding hurt.

"He told us everything we need to know," said Michael. "Mr. Drews has the bear, and he's going to ship it to Europe tomorrow."

"Well, we're going to have to stop him!" said Jennifer.

"I know," said Michael. "Now, when we get to town, we'll call your mom and ask if I can stay at your house tonight," he said at last. "Then, we'll call the school and I'll go and ask Mr. Drews for the bear."

"But, Michael, he wouldn't sell it to Mr. Grady. Why would he just give it to you?"

"He probably won't," said Michael. "But I'm going to try."

"What if he says no?"

"Then—then I'll find some other way to get it."

"You mean just *take* it?" Jennifer sounded shocked.

"If I have to," Michael answered. "But don't worry, you don't have to have anything to do with it."

"Are you kidding?" said Jennifer. "I won't let you steal it alone."

"Thanks," said Michael, meeting her gaze directly. "But, Jennifer, remember, this is really serious. We don't have a choice. We have to do whatever it takes to get that bear. If we don't, the bear will be lost forever. Then, just like Billy Merina, I'll be killed!"

CHAPTER 13

BY the time Michael and Jennifer got to Silverbell it was early evening and the sidewalks were crowded with people going home from work and doing last-minute shopping.

They chained their bikes to a rack in the town square, called Jennifer's mom, then crossed to Mr. Drews's shop.

The antique store was just as it had been before— dark, dusty, and crowded. There was no sign of Mr. Drews. "Hello?" Michael called out after he stepped through the door and set the bell jangling.

After a moment the old man came tottering out of the back room. "You two again?" he said with a scowl. "What do you want this time?"

"We—uh, we came to talk to you," said Jennifer.

"Well?" said Mr. Drews. "What is it? I'm closing."

"Well, you see, we're from the Chilleen Academy," Jennifer said. "And we're studying western history in school."

"Western history?" said the old man, his voice more suspicious than ever. "When you were here before, you said you were doing a play."

"The play is for our history class," said Michael quickly. "The main thing we're interested in is the early history of the West. We've been studying the ancient people of Phantom Valley. There's a story that they had a statue of a bear with one claw on each foot."

Mr. Drews suddenly frowned, but he didn't say anything.

"We're trying to find the bear," Michael went on. "It's really important. It's possible that the bear statue could save someone's life."

Mr. Drews remained silent. Then his face got red. "What does that have to do with me?" he shouted.

"We were wondering if you had anything like that in your shop," said Jennifer.

"No!" said Mr. Drews. "Even if I did, why would I tell you?"

It was obvious. Mr. Drews wouldn't admit he had the statue. Michael whispered to Jennifer. "Plan B," he said. He turned back to Mr. Drews. "Thanks anyway," he said. "I guess we'll just look around for a few minutes."

"Look all you want," said Mr. Drews. "But you won't find any bear."

It was nearly six, closing time. For ten minutes Michael and Jennifer secretly searched on opposite sides of the store. Jennifer rummaged around in the back, and Michael hovered near the front. He was nervous that someone would come in and ruin their plan. No one did.

"Get along now," Mr. Drews said gruffly. "I've got to close up."

"Okay," said Michael, standing beside the front door. He opened the door as if he were about to leave. Just to the left, inside the door, was a large black and gold Chinese screen.

"Thanks for letting us look," said Jennifer. She started for the door too, but hadn't gotten far when she purposely tripped and fell against a table piled high with old magazines. "Oops!"

The table and magazines went crashing to the floor.

"Look what you've done!" cried Mr. Drews, running to the table.

Mr. Drews bent down to pick up the magazines, his back to the door. Michael let the front door swing shut and stepped behind the Chinese screen, squatting down.

Jennifer glanced at the screen to make sure Michael was hidden. Then she said to Mr. Drews, "I'm so sorry! Let me help you clean it up."

"Leave me alone!" cried Mr. Drews. "You've done enough already! Just go, like your friend did!"

With another apology, Jennifer left the store.

From behind the screen, Michael heard Mr. Drews grumbling as he picked up the magazines. After a few minutes the old man went into the back room, then returned, clicked off all the lights except one, and left, locking the front door.

Michael waited till the sun went down, then scooted into the back room. It was a tiny office and, as Michael had hoped, had a window looking out onto the back alley. He unlocked and opened the window, then poked his head out. "Psst, Jennifer!" he called in a loud whisper.

Jennifer came running. "We did it!" she said with a grin as Michael helped her up and in through the window.

Michael locked the window before turning on his flashlight. "Finding the things won't be easy," he said. "This place is crammed with stuff."

"Let's split up," suggested Jennifer. "You look for the bear, and I'll look in Billy's things for the page that was torn out of your textbook."

While Jennifer went into the main shop, Michael quickly searched through the things in the office. He poked inside desk drawers and a small closet, but he found only some papers and pencils, a clock radio, and a raincoat.

Disappointed, he joined Jennifer in the other room. She was looking through some things on a shelf near the front of the store. "These are Billy Merina's things," she said. "I found his name on a box of toy soldiers. The only books here are ordinary schoolbooks. No papers at all."

"Maybe Linda Anne had the missing page," said Michael.

"Let's hope I can find her stuff," said Jennifer.

Michael went from shelf to shelf, table to table, checking for the statue of the bear. The shop had figures of cats, dogs, and penguins; it had old vases, dishes, and candlesticks; pots, pans, books, and furniture, but nothing that resembled a bear.

It could be anywhere, Michael realized. *How am I going to find it in all this junk?*

"Michael, come over here," Jennifer whispered loudly. "I think I've found Linda Anne's things."

"Great," said Michael. He crossed to a big table against one of the side walls. Jennifer was holding her flashlight under her chin while she went through a box stuffed with papers. "This is hers, all right," Jennifer said, sounding excited. "See this? It's her autograph book."

The name on the front of the book was Linda Anne Rogers. There was quite a few papers and books in the box.

"It's going to take a while to go through all this," said Jennifer, lifting items out of the box one by one. "She really had a lot of books and stuff."

"I'll keep searching for the bear," said Michael, wandering over to a section of the store he hadn't explored yet. Then suddenly he heard it again—the noise like thunder. It was so loud that he couldn't hear anything else.

Roaarrr! it sounded in his ear. *Roaarrrr!*

"Jennifer," he whispered when it died down. "Did you hear anything?"

"No," she said. "Just you walking around."

The sound grew louder again then, echoing in his head.

The roaring is just for me, Michael realized. *I'm the only one who can hear it.* He discovered that the noise was louder against the far wall. He moved toward it as if being pulled. The roaring grew louder, louder. *It's as if it's guiding me*, he thought.

The sound led him to the part of the room that was cluttered with desks, chairs, sofas, and other antique furniture.

Unbelievably the roar was even louder now. He could feel it vibrating in every bone of his body, calling him to come closer.

Roaarrrr. Roaarrrr!

The roar seemed to be coming from a little table in the very corner of the room—a table covered with a pink cloth. Curious, Michael reached out to the table. The roar was deafening now.

He pulled the cloth off the table, and could see it wasn't a table at all. It was an antique cabinet with wooden doors.

All at once the roaring stopped.

Slowly he reached out to open the cabinet doors. There was a hollow click as the door sprang open. Michael aimed his flashlight inside the cabinet. There, in the very back, was a green cardboard shoe box.

After reaching for the box, he pulled the lid off. Inside was something wrapped in brown paper. Carefully Michael unwrapped it, then put it in the beam from his flashlight.

It was the statue of the bear. It was carved from dark, polished stone, and looked exactly like the picture in the book. The bear was standing on its hind legs, its front paws in the air, its mouth open. On each of its paws was a single long claw.

Michael reached for the statue. As his finger touched the hard stone, he felt an electric shock. He was about to call to Jennifer that he'd found the bear when she called to him.

"Michael!" she said excitedly. "I've found it! I found the missing page!" She ran across the room, a piece of yellowed paper fluttering in her hand. "Linda Anne had it, just as we thought! It was folded up inside her jewelry box." She held out the paper, then saw what he was holding. "Is that—" she said.

"It's the bear," he said.

"Wonderful!" she cried. "You found it! You've got both things now! Now you can end the curse!"

"I know," said Michael. "All I have to do now is go back to the cave!"

"I'm so happy!" said Jennifer. "Come on. Let's get out of here."

Michael rewrapped the bear in the brown paper and stuck it in his pack along with the page of yellowed paper. "We'd better go out the back way so nobody will see us," he said. "And then we'll—" he broke off.

From the office came a loud scraping sound, followed by a crash, and then the tinkle of breaking glass.

Someone was coming in through the office window.

CHAPTER 14

MICHAEL and Jennifer froze. A moment later there was another crash and then the sound of something heavy being moved.

Jennifer grabbed Michael's hand. "We're going to get caught! What are we going to do?" she whispered.

"Get down!" whispered Michael. He and Jennifer ducked down behind the cabinet.

"Who could it be?" Jennifer asked in a shaky whisper. "Do you think the police saw us in here?"

"The police don't break windows," said Michael. "It must be a burglar."

Tap—tap—Now they could hear someone slipping in through the window. A moment later heavy footsteps sounded in the room they were hiding in.

Michael gripped Jennifer's hand and held his breath. *Please go away*, he thought. *Whoever you are, go away!*

The footsteps moved farther into the room. Michael peeked over the cabinet, but all he could see was a shadow, the shadow of a very large person.

The intruder turned on a flashlight and began to sweep it around the room. Michael and Jennifer scrunched as close to the floor as they could get.

Suddenly the intruder stopped. Only his flashlight swept the room. The next thing Michael knew, the bright light was shining directly in his face, blinding him.

"So it's you!" said a deep, menacing voice. "Come out of there!"

His heart racing, Michael stood up. Now that the light was no longer in his eyes, he could see that the intruder was—

"Mr. Grady!" cried Jennifer. "What are *you* doing here?"

"I'm just—um—checking on the place for Drews," said Mr. Grady. "And it looks like I've caught two young burglars."

"You're not checking for Mr. Drews!" said Michael, suddenly angry. "We heard you breaking in!"

Mr. Grady shrugged. "So what if I did?" he said. "We're all in this together."

"Actually, we were just leaving," said Michael, walking casually toward the back room.

"Not so fast!" said Mr. Grady, his voice even rougher and more menacing. Michael felt his heart beating faster. "What's this?" said the big man, pointing to the shoe box.

"This?" said Jennifer and grabbed it from the top of the cabinet where Michael had left it. "It's—well, it's a shoe box."

"It's more than that!" cried Mr. Grady. "What's in it?" He grabbed for the box. Instinctively, Jennifer pulled it out of his way and stepped behind a table. "Nothing's in it!" she said.

"I know better!" Mr. Grady said. "I've seen it before! It's the shoe box with the bear in it! Give it to me!"

Michael realized Mr. Grady thought the bear was still in the empty shoe box. As long as he didn't find out the bear was in Michael's pack, the statue would be safe. "Keep the box away from him, Jennifer!" Michael cried, understanding her tricky plan.

"Stop it!" shouted Mr. Grady. "That's mine! You have no idea how valuable it is!"

"I thought you wanted it for a museum!" said Jennifer.

"That's what I meant," said Mr. Grady. "Now, come on, let me have it!" Grady tried to get to Jennifer, but the shop was so crowded and he was so heavy that he could hardly squeeze through most of the aisles.

Michael started to run, then fell against a tall bookshelf that was jammed with books from the floor to the ceiling. For a moment the bookcase teetered as if it would fall, and it gave Michael an idea. "Throw it to me!" he called to Jennifer.

Jennifer threw the shoe box. Michael caught it and

stood directly in front of the bookcase. "Over here!" he called to Mr. Grady, holding up the box.

"Why, you—" said Mr. Grady and ran to that side of the store. Michael stayed where he was.

"You want it so much?" said Michael. "You can have it!" He dropped the box, then ran to the side of the bookcase. He pushed as hard as he could, toppling the bookcase and burying the shoebox under hundreds of books.

"No!" shrieked Mr. Grady. He lunged for the buried box.

Michael didn't wait to see when he'd dig it out. "Go, Jennifer!" he shouted. "Run!"

CHAPTER 15

MICHAEL and Jennifer ran to the office, opened the broken window, and climbed out. They raced down the alley and across to the town square where their bikes were chained.

Jennifer stopped at the edge of the square and looked back, panting, at Mr. Drews's shop. "There's no sign of Mr. Grady," she said.

"Don't worry," said Michael. "By the time he finds out the shoe box is empty, we'll be long gone."

They climbed on their bikes and began pedaling out of Silverbell. Just outside of town, Michael slowed down at the narrow side road that led to the cave. "Go on home, Jennifer," he said. "I'm taking the bear up to the cave."

"But it'll be night!" said Jennifer. "It could be dangerous."

"It might be more dangerous to wait."

"Then I'll go with you," she said, her face very pale.

"Thanks anyway," said Michael. "But I think it'll be better if you don't come. This is something I need to do alone."

Jennifer looked as if she wanted to argue, but she backed down and only nodded. She began pedaling along Silverbell Road in the direction of Chilleen and her family's ranch.

Michael took a deep breath and started riding toward the cave.

The crescent moon was bright, and the road to Wild Horse Canyon stretched out clearly in front of him. Both sides of the road were thickly lined with pine trees and bushes. As he pedaled, Michael could feel the weight of the idol inside his pack. *It won't be long now,* he thought. *Soon you'll be back where you belong.*

He had gone a couple of miles when the moon disappeared behind a cloud and the wind began to kick up. At the same time Michael became aware of a strange sound—it was a kind of howling that seemed to come from all directions at once. *It's the curse again,* he thought. It was so dark that he could see nothing. Then all at once he saw, lining the road, hundreds of pairs of shiny eyes, all of them focused on him.

Trying not to think about the animals, he kept pedaling.

But now, up ahead in the road, a shadow appeared,

and then another and another. To the right he saw a coyote, to the left a couple of rabbits and a deer. There was a sudden *swooshing* noise above him, and he raised his eyes to see that the air was thick with flying things, bats, hawks, and owls, all of them circling above him.

The wind began to blow with more force, whipping against his face and making it hard to ride.

The creatures were all around him now, running as fast as he could ride, slowly moving in toward him, but not attacking.

He began to pedal faster.

The animals began to close in on him. He could smell them—hear their panting as they ran. Now the coyotes began to howl. Above him, the hawks and the owls began to screech.

Whoosh! A hawk dived just in front of him, so close it brushed his hair.

Ay-ay-ay-ay! One of the coyotes jumped at him. Michael swerved and almost lost control of his bike. Just before he did, he managed to regain his balance.

His heart was pounding so hard he could hardly breathe. He was going as fast as he could, and yet he forced himself to go faster. *Think about riding*, he told himself. *Just concentrate on that.*

Up ahead he could see the outline of the cliffs of Wild Horse Canyon. But the animals were closer than ever. Another huge bird swooped down, and its long claws caught in his jacket. For a horrifying moment Michael thought he would be pulled off his bike.

He twisted away and shook his arm to get rid of the hawk. As the hawk flew away, a kind of whirlwind appeared ahead of him. At first he thought it was dust kicked up by the wind, but then he realized it was a swarm of bees.

He didn't have any choice. He made a sharp right, swerving around the swarm, keeping his head down to protect his face. He felt only one or two stings on his neck and face.

Just keep pedaling, he thought. *Just keep going. It's only a little way now.*

The bee stings burned. Then he felt something nip at his left foot. He kicked out and something nipped at his other foot. He kicked and swerved, trying to get away. He was almost free when a large deer appeared in the road just ahead of the bike.

"No!" he cried, but it was too late. The bike flew out from under him and Michael fell, hard, to the road. He took a moment to catch his breath, then looked up. All the animals were around him. Slowly they moved in on him. Deer, coyotes, rabbits, squirrels, a mountain lion. Even the gentlest of animals were in the circle. Their mouths were open, showing sharp teeth below gleaming yellow eyes. Up above, the bats and the birds circled, dropping lower and lower.

Shakily, Michael stood up. He had never in his life been so terrified. The animals continued to move in on him, coming closer and closer. A chorus of howls and cries went up. His heart beat faster with every advancing step the animals took. The circle grew smaller. In another second, the animals would be on him, attacking him. Michael squeezed his eyes shut. He was trapped!

ROOOOOOAAAAAAR!

Michael quickly opened his eyes, expecting to see the coyotes or the mountain lion right on top of him. But the coyotes were backing away, their tails down between their legs. The mountain lion and all the other animals in the circle were retreating, scattering in different directions. The birds and bats were flying away, too. Surprised and confused, he glanced around. All the animals that had been chasing him were running off, as if they had all been frightened by something that was more powerful and stronger than all of them together.

He became aware of the roaring again. It was the same, but now hundreds of times louder. It was so loud it filled his mind. It was the roar, he knew, of the bear from the cave.

A large, dark shadow fell over the area. Michael slowly peeked behind him—and froze. Lumbering toward him, from across the canyon, was the shadow of the biggest animal he had ever seen. As it grew closer, he could see that it was an enormous black bear, the bear of the cave. Its eyes were yellow and its gaping mouth revealed sharp, cruel-looking teeth. It had one long claw on each paw.

Terrified, Michael knew that no matter what, he must return the idol of the bear to the cave. He took a deep breath, picked up his back pack, and began to run straight toward the climbing trail, running for his life. From the sounds, he could tell that the gigantic bear was after him. *Please*, he thought, *please let me make it*.

He climbed up the trail as the roaring sound continued and the earth began to shake. The bear got closer, then stopped for a moment. It stood up on its hind feet, threw back its head, and let out a long and terrifying roar. When it stopped roaring, it dropped down on all fours, and gazed straight at Michael, and began to charge him.

The bear was so close he could hear its breathing. Now the birds began to dive-bomb him again. A hawk flew straight at his face. Michael rolled over on the trail, just in time to keep from getting his eyes pecked out.

He tried to scramble back up, to begin running again, but it was no use. In another second the bear would get him.

CHAPTER 16

"**N**O!" Michael screamed. He was near the top of the climbing trail, by the ledge that led into the cave.

The ground shook as the bear ran up the trail. Rocks and dirt were falling all around. Michael studied the narrow ledge as pieces of it broke off and fell into the canyon below.

The bear was just a few feet behind Michael now.

He had no choice. Taking a deep breath, Michael hitched his pack high onto his shoulder and inched out onto the ledge. It shook beneath his feet with every step the bear took. He started to slip, but regained his footing by grasping an exposed tree root.

Now the bear was at the top of the trail and starting to climb onto the ledge. The rocky ledge quivered. For a moment Michael was afraid it would collapse.

His heart pounding, he looked back and saw the bear still coming after him. Because the bear was so large and the ledge was so narrow, it had to slow down.

Directly ahead, Michael saw a dark space. The cave! He pulled his flashlight off his belt, then ducked into the dark entrance. Outside he could hear the bear sniffing for him as it drew closer.

He had to return the idol and say the words before the bear reached him.

He raced to the back of the cave, to the nook where the idol should be. His hands shaking, he reached inside his pack to pull out the statue. He was almost finished unwrapping the brown paper that covered it when the bear roared again. He couldn't help jumping. The statue slid from his hands and rolled across the cave floor.

"Noooo!" Michael wailed. He dived for the statue and picked it up. It wasn't cracked or harmed in any way. Holding his breath and trying to keep his hands steady, he started to place it inside the nook. But now there was a new problem. The statue was too big!

Maybe this is the wrong cave! Michael thought in panic. But no, it had to be the right one, he realized. Moving very slowly, he tried again. Gently, firmly, he pushed the statue into the nook. It just fit with no room left over. By pushing carefully, he was able to ease it all the way into the space. When it reached the back, it clicked into place.

At that moment the bear roared again. Michael had been so busy with the statue, he'd almost forgotten it.

"I've put the idol back!" he screamed into the darkness. But the bear only roared in response. He could feel the floor of the cave shake as the big beast got closer and closer.

The words, Michael told himself. *You've got to say the words*. Replacing the statue was only the first step toward ending the curse.

He reached into his pack and pulled out the page that Jennifer had given him back in the antique shop. He shone the flashlight on the page. There they were, the words that would save his life. He took a deep breath, prepared to recite the words.

Before he could get one word out, the entire cave shook. Michael looked up and froze. There, at the entrance to the cave, stood the bear on its hind legs.

The bear threw back its head and roared again, then dropped down and bounded into the cave, straight at Michael.

"*Teglet!*" Michael shouted into the gloom.

Roooaarrrr! The bear bounded closer.

"*Noaj!*" Michael continued reading the strange words. His hands were shaking so badly he could hardly hold the flashlight beam steady on the page. "*Enaj!*" he went on. "*Trebor, mellepyr!*" He was shouting the words at the top of his voice. The cave shook with the echoes of his words and the roaring of the bear.

He shouted the last word on the page: "*Teglet!*"

Suddenly the cave became silent. Completely silent.

There was no sign of the bear. It had vanished. Michael was completely alone.

Outside, through the opening of the cave, he could see stars sparkling. The night was quiet and peaceful.

It's over, he thought. *The curse has ended.* He felt nothing but peace flow over him. Slowly he turned to look at the back of the cave. The idol of the bear was standing in its niche as if it had never been disturbed.

While Michael continued to watch, the idol began to glow, as if lit by a golden fire inside. A moment later the cave filled with a sweet humming.

Not knowing what to do, Michael continued to stare at the idol. The humming grew louder. After a moment the humming formed into words, words that Michael heard not through his ears but directly inside his head.

"Thank you," the humming said. "Thank you for restoring me to my rightful place."

The bear glowed even brighter. It was shining so brightly it almost hurt Michael's eyes.

"What do you want?" the humming voice asked him. "What do you desire most in all of the world?"

Michael was so surprised by the question that he said the first thing that popped into his head. "I want to stay at Chilleen!" he cried.

Instantly the humming stopped. A moment later the golden light surrounding the idol faded. Michael continued to stare at it until it became completely dark again.

I must have imagined it, he thought. *I must have imagined I saw the lights and heard the words.* Deep down, he knew he had not imagined them. He knew that the light had come from the spirit of the bear, and the words had been for him.

Michael was suddenly very tired, but there was one more thing he had to do. He scanned the page of words that had ended the curse. Then he reached into his back pocket and pulled out the other page, which he had ripped out of the book and taken with him. Why, he hadn't been sure at the time. Now he was glad he had. For one crazy moment he thought about reading the words over again, but he knew that would be stupid and dangerous. It would be far better to see it was all destroyed, destroyed forever.

He gathered some leaves and twigs from the floor of the cave, and placed them in a tiny hollow spot near the center of the cave. He lit a match and touched it to the leaves. When a small fire was burning, he placed the two pages on top of the flame and watched while they withered to ashes.

When there was nothing but black powder left, he heard the terrifying roar of the bear again. At the same instant the cave began to shake. Michael felt as if his heart had stopped. Had the bear come back? The roaring grew louder, and then dirt and small rocks began to fall from the roof of the cave.

It's a cave-in! he realized in sudden panic. Choking on the dust, he scrambled to his feet. The ground was shaking so hard he almost lost his balance. The roar had changed to a deep rumble. Dirt and rocks were falling all around him now. Holding his breath, Michael ran to the front of the cave.

The entire cave was shaking as Michael dived head

first out of the entrance and onto the ledge. A moment later with a deafening *whoosh* the cave collapsed. Clouds of dust filled the air. Facedown on the ledge, Michael dug his fingers into the dirt. He was afraid he would be thrown off the ledge or that the shaking would break it apart.

After many minutes the roaring died down and the ledge stopped shaking. Michael sat up and turned his head to the cave, blinking in surprise. Where the entrance had been, there was now nothing but rocks. There was no sign of the cave at all, no sign it had ever existed.

It was very late at night when Michael rode his bike onto the academy grounds. He decided not to disturb Jennifer and her family and to just go back to his room at school to sleep. On his ride home he kept an eye out for animals, but saw nothing but a rabbit, which ignored him, and an owl, hooting in a tree.

The nightmare is over, he told himself again.

But is it really?

There was one way to find out. Just ahead, he could make out the dark shape of the stables.

He knew that what he was about to do could be dangerous, but he had to know for sure. He hopped off his bike, leaned it against the barn door, and entered the stables. The familiar, friendly smell of warm hay and horses greeted him. Holding his breath, he walked over to the stall belonging to Duke.

He held out his hand and patted the animal on the head. Duke whinnied softly and nuzzled him.

A moment later Michael felt something brush against his leg. He looked down to see Rex, the stable dog, wagging his tail in greeting.

It's true, he thought. *It's over. The curse is gone forever.*

CHAPTER 17

"**D**ID you hear the news?" Luke sounded excited as he plopped his full breakfast tray down next to Michael's.

"What?" he said, hiding a yawn behind his hand.

"Our new cook, Mr. Grady, has been arrested!"

"You're kidding!" said Chubber.

Michael raised an eyebrow. "What happened?" he asked.

"It happened last night," said Luke. "It turns out he wasn't a cook at all—he was an art thief, and the police caught him in a store in Silverbell robbing the place."

"I thought something was different," said Chubber, peering at his scrambled eggs. "My eggs taste exactly like eggs this morning. I wonder who cooked them."

"Someone said Mr. Elias is cooking until he can hire

a new cook," said Luke. "But just imagine, a criminal was working right here at Chilleen, and we didn't even know it."

Michael didn't say a thing. He knew he had to keep everything that had happened a secret, just for him and Jennifer to know. He had been right. Mr. Grady hadn't been a cook—or an archaeologist either.

"I wonder what will happen to Mr. Grady," said Luke.

"Maybe they'll send him to jail cooking school," joked Chubber.

"Very funny," said Michael. Then he started to giggle. A moment later everyone was laughing.

As Michael was about to take his empty tray to the conveyer belt, Mr. Elias poked his head into the dining room. "Michael?" he called out. "Mrs. Danita wants to see you in her office."

Uh-oh, he thought. Had Mrs. Danita, the headmistress, found out about the break-in at Mr. Drews's antique store?"

"Come in, Michael," said the motherly headmistress.

"Good morning, Mrs. Danita," said Michael. For some reason he always felt a little nervous around the woman, even though all the kids agreed she was nice.

"Please have a seat," Mrs. Danita said. "Mr. Elias tells me your scholarship will run out at the end of this semester."

"Yes, it will," said Michael, remembering all at once that he wouldn't be staying at Chilleen.

Mrs. Danita picked up a thick manila envelope from the top of her desk. "Well, I have what I think is good news for you," she said.

For a moment Michael just stared at her. *Good news? What could it be?*

"I received this unexpectedly," Mrs. Danita went on, pointing at the envelope. "It's a donation from one of our alumni—a considerable amount of money to create a new scholarship. I have complete control over awarding it."

Michael continued to listen, hardly daring to breathe.

"Because you have done so well here, I have decided to award the scholarship to you, if you'll accept it."

"If I'll accept it—" Michael was so happy and excited he could hardly find the words to answer. "You bet I will, Mrs. Danita," he said. "I want to stay here more than anything!"

"Good," said Mrs. Danita. "Then it's settled. And I'm so happy for you, Michael. This is such good luck."

"Yes, it is," he said. Deep inside he knew it wasn't luck. He knew the scholarship was a gift from the bear. A way of saying thank you.

About the Author

LYNN BEACH was born in El Paso, Texas, and grew up in Tucson, Arizona. She is the author of many fiction and nonfiction books for adults and children.